Norby and the Queen's Necklace

NORBY AND THE QUEEN'S NECKLACE

Janet and Isaac Asimov

Walker and Company
New York, New York

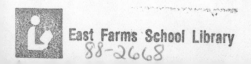

First published in the United States of America in 1986 by the Walker Publishing Company, Inc.

Published simultaneously in Canada by Beaverbooks, Limited, Pickering, Ontario.

Library of Congress Cataloging-in-Publication Data

Asimov, Janet.
  Norby and the queen's necklace.

  Summary: Fourteen-year-old Jeff Wells and his robot friend Norby are suddenly transported back to 1785 in France, where they become involved with a priceless necklace and royal politics.
  1. France—History—18th century—Juvenile fiction.
[1. France—History—18th century—Fiction. 2. Robots—Fiction. 3. Space and time—Fiction] I. Asimov, Isaac, 1920-   . II. Title.
PZ7.A836Nn   1986   [Fic]   86-11120
ISBN 0-8027-6659-5
ISBN 0-8027-6660-9 (lib. bdg.)

Printed in the United States of America

10 9 8 7 6 5 4 3 2 1

To Marg and Bill Atwood, with thanks.

1

Dangerous Play

"Jefferson Wells, actor?" The museum guard scowled and barred the doorway. "So *you* say. Where's your identification?"

"I haven't got it," said Jeff earnestly. "Fargo didn't give me one. That's Farley Gordon Wells, who's playing the part of the King. He's my brother. I'm in the skit, too—gentlemen-in-waiting—and I'm first on the stage. . . ."

"I don't care who you are or what you're supposed to do. You've got to have identification. That Queen's necklace we have is valuable and no one gets in who isn't authorized. And even if you had identification, you can't bring in your barrel. It would have to be checked."

The domed lid of the barrel, complete with metal brim, popped up to reveal half a head with two eyes glaring with anger at the guard. Facing Jeff on the other side of the head were two more eyes, looking just as angry.

"I go where Jeff goes, you numbskull!" The metallic voice seemed to come from the lid. As Fargo always said, Norby—the small robot that looked like a barrel—always talked through his hat.

The guard reddened and Jeff interposed quickly. "This is the teaching robot for the whole cast," he said. "His name is Norby and he's very temperamental, so you'll have to excuse him. We're all speaking French and Norby makes sure we get it right. He's absolutely necessary to the skit. So you see, *I've* got to get in. And *Norby*'s got to get in."

"That's right," said Norby sounding smug. "This skit is being put on before an audience of Federation dignitaries, in case you don't know it, Mr. Whatever-your-name-is." Norby's legs telescoped out of his barrel body, so Jeff put him down.

Rocking back and forth on his two-way feet, Norby telescoped out both of his arms, grabbed Jeff's hand and said, "If we don't get in, the skit can't go on and the Queen's necklace, which is the museum's newest acquisition, can't be publicized. And everyone will want to bounce you off the wall! So just let us pass."

He tried to walk forward, pulling at a rather reluctant Jeff, who preferred to make his point by reason.

The guard threw himself in front of them, arms outstretched. "No, you don't. It doesn't matter what you say. No identification, no entrance. Those are my instructions. And it especially goes for fresh kids and barrels."

The guard was not a very tall man, and Jeff was nearly six feet tall, even though he was only fourteen. He looked down at the guard and said quietly, "Do I look like a fresh kid? I'm a Space Cadet and I'm in the skit along with my brother, Fargo, and his fiancée, Albany Jones, who's a police lieutenant and the daughter of the mayor of Manhattan. I'm afraid they're all going to have something to say to you if you don't let me pass this minute."

"Yes? Well, here comes Mayor Jones. Talk to *him*, you fresh kid."

A big man in dress tunic stepped out of an official air car at

2

the foot of the broad steps leading to the front door of the Metropolitan Museum of Art in the nation of Manhattan (now part of the Terran Federation).

Mayor Leo Jones had a massive head with a shock of sandy hair that made him resemble a good-humored but determined lion. He bounded up the steps and clapped Jeff on the shoulder. "What's wrong, Jeff, old man? Why are you hanging about out here and keeping Marie Antoinette waiting?"

The guard gulped and backed off, but Jeff said, "No problem, Mr. Mayor. I was a little late and was just about to present my identification."

"Forget it. You're with me," said the mayor.

Norby made a sardonic little bye-bye motion at the guard with one of his hands and marched ahead into the great hall and through the Egyptian wing with an air of owning the place, while Jeff and the mayor followed at a more sedate pace.

Despite his four eyes, Norby was moving too rapidly to get out of the way of the Holovision Director as she charged out of the auditorium.

There was a collision, and the director, a formidably large woman, said, "Oof," rubbed her bruised knee, and glared first at Norby and then at Jeff.

"Jefferson," she said, "you're late, and I don't want you letting that so-called teaching robot running about on his own. He's a menace! Are you aware this show is live? We have to start on time." She looked quickly at her watch. "You have to get into your costume and makeup *now*."

"I'm sorry," muttered Jeff. "I'll do it as fast as I can." He hauled Norby off to the dressing room where he found Fargo

3

already elegant in an elaborate wig and a costume that was a faultless fit. Too faultless, because it was skintight and he clearly would be unable to sit in it—or even move, perhaps.

Fargo greeted Jeff with an abrupt, "Well, what kept *you?*" and then turned away in order to continue arguing with the museum's Curator of History, a thin, anxious man.

"How can I tie the blasted ribbons around her neck when I'm wearing these tight lace gloves with only part of my fingers sticking out? I can hardly move them."

The curator sighed, "It's the director's orders. She insists on absolute authenticity of costume—which is ridiculous since the entire skit is fiction. Marie Antoinette probably never tried on the necklace. And if she had, she probably would have wanted to keep it. That would have been in keeping with her thoughtlessness and would have made her almost as unpopular as the loss of the necklace did. Obviously the novel by Alexander Dumas had it all wrong—"

Fargo interrupted. "I have no time to worry about the historical accuracy of the skit. I need practical help. Can't you fix a large simple clasp on the necklace so I can slip one end into the other with a nice click and have it done? How can I maneuver slippery ribbons into a knot that will hold while I'm wearing these gloves?"

The curator looked horrified. "A *clasp* on the Queen's necklace? We'd be a laughing stock! The whole point of the skit is to publicize this valuable acquisition—"

"It's not the original," protested Fargo. "As I understand it, the original no longer exists. This is just a paste replica."

"Even so," said the curator patiently, "it is an *exact* paste replica and has enormous historical value. It would be unthinkable to fiddle with it. Haven't you seen it? The necklace is an open metal bib covered with diamonds—or rather, simulated diamonds. Fastened to metal loops at each side are ribbons that are tied about the neck. That's the way it was designed, and that's the way it must be shown. No clasps!"

"Ridiculous!" said Fargo.

"What's ridiculous," snapped the curator, "is a tall police-woman playing a short Marie Antoinette and a skinny fellow like you playing a fat Louis the Sixteenth. *That's* what's ridiculous!" The curator stalked out, slamming the door behind him.

Fargo shrugged at Jeff. "Such a fuss over a skit to make publicity for the museum. And you should see the security over the necklace—as though anyone would want to steal something that has only historical value."

Jeff had now struggled into his costume and was trying not to sneeze while a young woman powdered his face and darkened his eyebrows.

A metallic grating sound issued from Norby. He was chuckling.

"Both of you look silly in satin and lace. Wouldn't you rather be in a play about the French Revolution than do this fictitious renunciation scene? Read Dickens—"

"Norby," said Fargo, "don't give me any trouble. The museum wants to publicize the necklace, not the replica of a guillotine."

"But everyone knows this replica necklace is only junk used by the jewelers, Boehmer and Bossange, as a model to show to the possible buyers of the real diamond necklace, which was stolen, broken up, and the individual stones sold. It's gone. Why the fuss about the replica?"

5

"Humans are sentimental about history," said Jeff, trying to adjust his too-small wig. "This paste replica is the only physical reminder of the Queen's necklace and it has a romantic story, too. It turned up in the trunk of a family whose ancestors had emigrated from France, first to England and later to the United States. There was all kinds of excitement about identifying and authenticating it and more excitement about *which* museum would get it. Having the Metropolitan acquire it was a great victory for Manhattan."

"It probably cost a great deal and it isn't worth it," said Norby. "I've seen pictures of it and I think it's ugly. The metal holding the stones is dark. It's not silver, the way the real diamond necklace is supposed to have been. I still think the beheading of Marie Antoinette would be more interesting."

"No beheading for *my* Marie Antoinette," said Fargo, shaking his head and causing his heavy powdered wig to fall off and land at the feet of the director, who had just barged in.

"Put that back on!" she bellowed (her natural tone of voice). "We're ready to begin. The necklace will be taken out of its security container as soon as you're backstage."

Fargo said politely, "Would you mind picking up the wig? I can't bend in this stupid costume."

Jeff picked up the wig quickly before the director could make up her mind whether or not to perform the menial service.

The director looked Fargo up and down and smiled toothily. "I must say you're charming in this costume."

"Too tight," said Fargo.

6

"Exactly," said the director. "Come along."

Backstage, Albany stood next to Fargo, her powdered wig high and looped with jewels, the bodice of her gown cut low.

"You look stunning," whispered Fargo, "much too pretty to go to the guillotine."

"Don't forget," said Albany, "the King loses his head first."

"I already have," said Fargo grinning.

Jeff said, "Norby, what's the matter?" for Norby had suddenly extruded his sensor wire from his hat.

"I don't know. They've taken the fake necklace out of the security container and this is the first time I've been able to sense it. There's something odd about it."

"Silence!" shouted the director, shoving Jeff onto the stage.

The curtain rose and Jeff stared straight ahead, trying not to think of the glittering audience of city officials before him, or of the holovision cameras. The director's music synthesizer was giving out what was supposed to be 18th century French music. Then suddenly there was a trumpet blast. Jeff pulled open a door of the stage set, bowing as Fargo entered. Fargo walked forward carefully as he tried to keep his elaborate wig in balance.

"Ah, my faithful Jacques," said Fargo in Old French. "The Queen will arrive at any moment. She does not know I have a present for her."

He held up the little jewel box, covered with purple velvet, and Jeff's sharp ears could almost hear the distant squeak of the simultaneous translation into Terran Basic

7

through the earpieces affixed to each member of the audience.

Out of the corner of his eye he could see Norby's domed hat peeping around a backstage curtain in the wings. Norby's hand was waving at him.

Then it seemed as though someone had pulled Norby back. And soon afterward, Albany swept past the back curtain and through the open door as Jeff bowed low again.

Jeff could not hear the opening dialogue between King and Queen because Norby was trying to speak to him softly through the thin painted back wall of the set.

"Jeff," came Norby's voice. "It's something bad—dangerous—"

"Shut up!" came the hoarse whisper of the director.

"Let me tie the necklace around you, my love," said Fargo to Albany as he opened the box and displayed its contents. "Your beauty will enhance the diamonds."

"But we can't afford it," said Marie Antoinette, with her hands behind her back, not daring to touch the necklace lest she weaken. "France cannot afford it. We drove ourselves nearly into bankruptcy helping the Americans in their fight against Great Britain."

"My ministers said it was worth it to weaken Great Britain. Is it not a beautiful necklace?"

"Incredibly beautiful, but I do not wish it."

"Is it that you object because it was originally made for my grandfather in order that he might give it to the Dubarry woman?"

The Queen's nose tilted higher into the air. "I have no love for the Dubarry, but the necklace never touched her. No, it's my concern for France that stops me. Send the necklace back

8

to Boehmer and Bossange. Perhaps someone else will pay the one million six hundred thousand *livres*."

"But I must see it on you, even if only once," said the King.

Jeff's nose was itching, but he couldn't scratch it, and it seemed to him that backstage Norby was still trying to make him hear some warning.

"Ah, well. Just once," said Marie Antoinette, stepping into the brightest light on stage as Fargo took out the necklace and handed the box to Jeff, who put it on a side table.

Holding the heavy necklace by its smooth and slippery ribbons, Fargo advanced to the Queen and, of course, the ribbons slipped through his fingers and the necklace fell to the floor.

"A sign from the angels that this was not meant to be," ad-libbed Fargo in his role as King. He made a negligent gesture as though the matter were of no importance, and bent down to pick up the necklace—forgetting that kings do not do that sort of thing.

There was a loud, tearing sound and Fargo suddenly paled. Jeff wondered why his twenty-four-year-old brother should look so upset. And then he saw that the seat of Fargo's satin trousers had split neatly up the seam.

Fargo held the necklace irresolutely for a moment. He was supposed to tie it around Albany's neck from the front, while she faced the audience, but that would have meant displaying his backside, something he clearly did not intend to do. For a moment, he hesitated. Then he said, "Ho, Jacques, tie this necklace around the Queen's neck. I feel clumsy today."

An anguished but suppressed howl rose from behind the

scenes as the Curator of History witnessed the terrible mistake of having any male who was not the King touch the Queen in so intimate a fashion.

Jeff ignored it and took the necklace from Fargo, who grabbed Jeff's hand for a moment.

In that moment Jeff heard in his mind a telepathic message from his brother—a telepathy made possible by their earlier adventures in space.

——Jeff, you've got to tie the blasted thing because I've split my trousers.

——I know, Your Majesty.

——Don't be funny, and tie it right.

Jeff approached the Queen respectfully, quite certain she had heard the seam split and knew what was going on. One could always trust Albany's intelligence.

What one couldn't trust was the necklace. Jeff placed it on Albany's chest and tried to tie the ribbons behind her neck. But they wouldn't tie. However he knotted them, the ribbons started to give as soon as he let go. Fargo had moved to the other side of Albany and was trying, uselessly, to help.

Jeff continued to fumble while Albany stared over his shoulder at the audience and improvised a patter of French conversation that seemed to deal endlessly with the expenses of the crown and what she would like to buy for her little Trianon palace.

Jeff, desperate, noted that the two back tassels of the necklace seemed longer and sturdier than those in front. Each ended in a big diamond from which hung a bell-like arrangement with five connecting short chains of diamonds. It was very gaudy and Jeff felt himself beginning to agree with Norby that the necklace was ugly.

10

He could hear some slight tittering from the audience. He was taking too long. Breathing deeply, he took the two back tassels and looped them over each other, first once—not firm enough yet to hold the necklace in place—and then—

"Jeff! Wait!" Norby's voice was clearly audible.

But the audience was beginning to laugh and both Fargo and Albany seemed unable to continue. Jeff *couldn't* wait.

Jeff looped the back tassels a second time and yanked them into a tight knot. Fargo was pulling, too. Between that and the diamonds at the end of each tassel, the new knot would *have* to hold.

"Jeff," shouted Norby. "Don't do that!"

2
Into History

What Jeff realized first was that he wasn't on the stage at the Metropolitan Museum of Art.

The stage did not have an oriental carpet on the floor. Yet one was directly below Jeff's nose because he was lying on it. He turned his head and saw a high slit of a window and beyond it, rooftops silhouetted against what looked like the pale streaks of light in an early morning sky.

He rose to his feet and saw that he was in a small, dark room, lighted only by the window and the soft glow of an oil lamp on a heavy wooden desk.

"Ow! I think I've hit somebody," said Fargo.

"Where are we?" asked Albany. She was there, too. "And who's that?"

Lying unconscious near Fargo was a small man in brown costume, a necklace clutched in his left hand. A similar necklace, much shinier, had apparently fallen from his right hand. Albany picked it up.

"These look like real diamonds!" she said, crossing her long legs under the big skirt and rising with one athletic motion. "Have we found the real Queen's necklace?" It dangled from her hand, and in the daylight it was brighter than the dull replica necklace around her neck.

Jeff was studying a newspaper on the desk. It was French, but despite the archaic typeface and its generally ancient appearance, the paper itself seemed quite new. He said, "I think we've travelled through time somehow. If this newspaper is the real thing, we're in France, Paris probably, and this is the 18th century. In fact, if this is yesterday's newspaper, this is the morning of February 1, 1785, the day the necklace was delivered to Cardinal Rohan. He'd been led to believe that the Queen wanted him to buy it for her."

"Then that's Bossange. Or Boehmer," said Fargo, rising stiffly, the cloth of his underpants showing through the rip in his satin costume. "He's just knocked out, I hope. And where is that blasted robot of yours, Jeff? He can go through time. So I suppose he's responsible for all this."

"I'm sorry, Fargo. Norby's not here. He'd be all over me if he were."

"He *must* be here. How would we have travelled through time without him? And why here, I wonder? And why now? I tell you I'll scoop out that little monster's insides and use his barrel to store mothballs."

"But, Fargo," said Albany, "Norby wasn't on stage with us when we left. He couldn't have moved us through time without making physical contact with us, could he?"

"Actually," said Jeff, "he was trying to warn me not to tie the back tassels of the necklace. Is it possible that what we were fooling with was more than just a replica of the Queen's necklace? We were all three standing close together, in contact, and perhaps the replica was a time-travel device that was invented by someone, somewhere, sometime."

Fargo leaned against the desk and flicked at the lace on his wrists. "If we're going to imagine a mysterious time-travel device, we might as well imagine magic. That would be more fun."

"Scientists say that magic is a name we use for something we don't understand," said Jeff. "Albany, maybe it would be better if you took off the necklace."

"But if it brought us here, we'd better hang on to it tightly," said Albany. "How would we get home without it as a time-travel device? And wouldn't it be nice to go back home with the *authentic* Queen's necklace? That would surprise the museum authorities right out of their socks." She held the real diamonds next to the paste stones she was wearing. "See the difference?"

"The jeweler's waking up, assuming he *is* the jeweler," said Fargo. "Shall I hit him a little bit to keep him unconscious?"

"Don't," said Jeff. "If you injure him, history may be changed. And that goes double if we try to return with the real necklace."

"It's probably changed already," said Fargo. "once we fall into the 18th century, practically anything we do will change history. And what *will* we do? I'll have to brush up on sword play. Or maybe that will go out of fashion with the French Revolution coming in only four years. And after that there will be that young soldier named Napoleon, who rose to become Emperor of France."

The jeweler began to call out weakly, "Bossange! Bossange!"

"This one is Boehmer then," said Jeff.

While the little jeweler, Boehmer, struggled to sit up, his eyes still closed, the replica necklace in his hand slipped to the carpet.

14

Albany let out a startled cry and Jeff saw with horror that the replica necklace had begun to wriggle like a snake across the carpet toward her.

"That's the same thing you're wearing," said Fargo. "I think I get it now. This is an example of one object at two different time periods and it's struggling to join itself!"

Still holding the real diamond necklace, Albany touched the replica tied around her neck. She stepped hastily away from the crawling replica on the floor.

"It's horrifying watching that thing crawl," she said. "I think I'd feel safer somewhere else." And with that she suddenly seemed to blink out. The replica necklace she'd been wearing was gone. The diamond necklace she'd been holding was gone. Now only the other replica remained.

Fargo rushed to the spot where Albany had been standing. "Where did she go? How?"

The replica necklace on the floor stopped moving the moment Albany vanished, and now lay still on the floor as if it had never tried to reach itself.

Boehmer opened his eyes, looked at his empty hands, and shouted in German-accented French. "Thieves! Help! Bossange! Thieves! We are being robbed!"

His partner, Bossange, entered the room with a pistol.

"We're American visitors—" began Fargo.

"They have stolen the necklace," shrieked Boehmer. "The real one. Bossange, hold the pistol ready. We will force them to give up what they have taken. I shall call the police. We must deliver the diamonds today. The cardinal will not be happy if we delay. Nor," and he looked at Fargo and Jeff with savagery in his eyes, "will the Queen of France. It's the Bastille for you."

15

And it was. Nor did Jeff and Fargo enjoy it, for the Bastille dungeons were dark, damp, and dirty. And they smelled terrible.

"If only Albany hadn't picked up the real diamonds," said Jeff. He spoke in Terran Basic, for there was another prisoner in the dungeon with them. "Then the jewelers would have no charge against us except breaking and entering. Now they think we threw the necklace out the window to a confederate."

Fargo sat down on a moldy bench. "If only she hadn't disappeared with the necklace. Or if only we had the slightest idea where she was. She's probably in a different time period altogether, I suppose."

"Maybe she went back to Manhattan," said Jeff. "*Our* Manhattan."

"Maybe," said Fargo. "But without the replica and without Norby, we can't go anywhere." He sighed. "I never thought that Space Command's top secret agent would go to the guillotine."

"You won't be guillotined," said Jeff as he stared at the third person in the room in an absent way—there didn't seem to be any use at this point in making friends. "The guillotine hasn't been invented yet."

"I don't remember much of the ancient history Norby tried to pour into me," said Fargo. "What happens instead? Do they hack off your head with an axe?"

"If you're an aristocrat, they do. If we can't convince them we're aristocrats, we're hanged. Or drawn and quartered. Or broken at the wheel."

"That doesn't sound like fun."

"It isn't," said Jeff. He shivered. He wasn't shivering

entirely at the thought of execution. Since it was indeed February 1, the room was cold.

The other prisoner of the room spoke up, "Pardon me, my friends. You speak a language to me unknown. Is it, then, that you do not speak French?"

Fargo said, "We are Americans, but we speak French." And he said it in French.

The other prisoner said, "Ah! Then shall we speak French? Permit me to introduce myself." He was a middle-aged man, but he was no bigger than a large child. "My name is Marcel Oslair and I am delighted to make your acquaintance. I have not much time for making acquaintances or for keeping them now, and I will not be fatiguing you with my presence for long. I am to be executed this afternoon."

For all that had happened since Fargo, Jeff, and Albany had been dropped into the jewelry shop of Boehmer and Bossange, it was still morning.

"We will be served our one meal of the day soon," Marcel continued, "and I am afraid that in spite of there being few prisoners in the Bastille right now, the food leaves much to be desired. May I have the pleasure of knowing your names, my dear sirs?"

"I'm Fargo Wells and this is my brother Jeff. But tell us, why are you going to be executed? You don't have the appearance of a desperate criminal."

"Alas, it is not necessary to be a desperate criminal to be executed, my friends. Or necessary even to be guilty. Mine is a sad story, for I am completely innocent of any crime." Marcel's smile lit his thin, dirty face like a lamp. "All prisoners say that, of course, but in my case it happens to be true. I come from a family of clockmakers, but you have

17

probably not heard of the Oslair clocks and automata if you are foreign spies—"

"Spies!" said Fargo indignantly.

"I crave pardon," said Marcel apologetically. "As you were being brought in, one of the guards told me I would have the honor of playing host to a pair of foreign spies. I took you to be Austrians, in league with our foreign queen."

"We are certainly not Austrians."

"I see then why I did not understand your language, for I speak a bit of German."

"We are Americans."

Marcel looked doubtful. "It is true I don't understand English, but how can you be Americans? Does not all the world know that Americans wear simple homespun clothes? And you do not have an American accent."

"Fargo," said Jeff impatiently, "let Marcel finish telling us why he's here." He turned to the little man. "When you say your family made automata, did you mean robots?"

"I do not know that word," said Marcel hesitantly. "Is it an English word?"

"Well, yes, in a way," said Jeff, reddening a bit. How could he forget that the word, robot, which was Czech in origin, would not be applied to mechanical men for another century and a third? "What I meant was, did your family make mechanical men?"

"Ah, yes, and ladies who played the harpsichord, and birds that laid eggs, and many other wonders. Some of the automata were life-sized and since I have always been small, I could get inside to work the machinery. Those were great days for my family, but alas, all of my people are gone now, and I am the last of the Oslairs." He shook his head sadly. "In a few hours I will be gone, too," he said.

18

"You have not yet told us how you come to be in the Bastille," Jeff said.

"You see, my friend, after I was left alone, I found no way of earning a living by myself and I was forced to sell the automata, one by one. Finally I had left but one goose and it caused my downfall."

"A mechanical goose?"

"Indeed. When my landlord grew importunate for his rent, I sold the goose, too, and, through misfortune, to a villain who filled the inside with stolen gold and shipped it to England. I was blamed both for the theft and the treachery of shipping French gold to another country. I had no bill of sale, and the man was a known criminal, though not to me. He vanished across the border. No one believed my story, and I had no family left to help me."

"Terrible," said Jeff. "Was there no trial?"

"But, of course there was," said Marcel. "We are not savages here. I was quickly convicted, however. The judges were not going to believe a little clockmaker when it was more important to show how efficient they were in convicting and punishing a criminal—whether he was a criminal or not. So now I must be ready to die. It is not so bad. I will be joining the rest of my family, perhaps, wherever they have gone. My dear father and mother—my younger brother—"

Fargo removed his heavy wig and used it as a pillow. He said, "Marcel, if we can think of a way of getting out of the Bastille, we will try to take you with us."

"My friend, you are most kind."

"But for now, I seem to have lost a night somewhere, and I must sleep a short while."

"Sleep well," said Marcel cheerfully.

Fargo could sleep anywhere and under any conditions,

and was soon snoring while Jeff continued to rack his brains for a way out.

"Marcel," he said softly, "why do you think Americans dress in homespun?"

"All the world knows it," said Marcel, puzzled at the question. "And they don't wear wigs."

Jeff removed his. It was uncomfortable anyway, and it was bad enough to be dressed in tight satin clothes.

Marcel nodded. "Cher papa does not approve of wigs."

"Your late father?"

"Ah, and you insist you are an American. Do you not know that the American ambassador, Benjamin Franklin, is called 'cher papa' by the ladies of the court?"

"Franklin! Yes, he must still be here in France! I forgot."

"Monsieur Franklin does not dress as you and your brother do," said Marcel.

"Could I see him, I wonder?"

"Alas, he is old and often ill. He rarely leaves his home in Passy."

"Where's that?"

"A short distance from Paris, on the way to Versailles."

"Could someone get there with a message in a short time?"

"Less than an hour with a horse," said Marcel.

Jeff ran to the door and yelled for the guard. "I demand to see Benjamin Franklin, my compatriot! There will be trouble with the United States of America if you don't send for him!"

No one answered, and Marcel laughed. "That new country you claim as your own is very small and weak, and in no condition to take offense at anything a great power like France might want to do to foreign spies."

"But I'm not a spy. I'm only fourteen."

"Old enough and big enough to be a soldier or a spy."

Jeff sat down next to Fargo and tried to think. If he couldn't talk to Franklin, the only hope was Norby, but could the robot respond? Did he still exist?

His back was against Fargo's back and the contact allowed the thought to cross over telepathically. Fargo yawned and said in Terran Basic, "I agree. Summon Norby. Perhaps the replica took Albany to Versailles. Perhaps it reacts to the way one is dressed. With Norby we'll be able to look for her there."

"I'm trying, but he's several centuries and almost five thousand kilometers away from us."

"He's your robot, Jeff. He tunes into you better than anyone. It's the only chance I see at the moment."

"But, Fargo, suppose our coming here has changed history and there's no Norby in the future, in our own time? Suppose *we* don't exist in our future either?"

"We exist here."

"But—"

"Jeff," said Fargo firmly. "Don't invent catastrophes. Let's pretend Norby exists, and you try to reach him. Besides, our clockmaker friend feels left out when we talk in Terran Basic."

"Sorry, Marcel," Jeff said in French. "I need to meditate— to sit in silence and think deeply. Do you know what I mean?"

"Certainly. I used to meditate while waiting for my father to give me the signal when I was inside the big automata. It made the waiting easier and made me calmer for any task ahead."

"That's what I need," said Jeff. "I have a very difficult task ahead." And he settled down to attempt it.

3
The Executioner's Block

The dank, grey walls of the Bastille seemed to close in on Jeff. It was so hard to concentrate. Reaching Norby seemed impossible, and after half an hour, he gave up.

He began pacing up and down the miserable chamber, while Fargo and Marcel, having nothing better to do, watched him, their eyes turning back and forth.

Jeff stopped suddenly. He had an idea.

"Fargo," he said, "there's a pen in my inside jacket pocket. Do you have any paper?"

"Paper? You're kidding. This stupid costume's so tight that I had to leave everything in the dressing room."

Jeff thought for a moment and decided he didn't need his inside pocket. He ripped it out and began to write on the material, which was white cotton because the museum had not thought it necessary to line the inside of the costume with satin.

"Is that English?" asked Marcel, looking on.

"Yes, it is," said Jeff.

"The pen writes even though you haven't dipped it in ink."

"An American invention," said Fargo smoothly. "News of it has not yet spread to other countries."

"Fascinating," said Marcel.

Looking over Jeff's shoulder, Fargo said, "What kind of

message is that? 'We must all hang together or, most assuredly, we shall all hang separately.' It doesn't mean anything."

"Franklin will recognize the words," said Jeff. "Now give me the top button from your waistcoat, Fargo. Mine aren't gold-colored."

"But they're only gold-colored plastic."

"Exactly why I want one to send to Franklin."

"My friends—the jailer is opening the door with our meal," said Marcel. "Can't you smell it?"

"Unfortunately, I can," said Fargo, removing his lace gloves and stuffing them into his waistcoat pocket. The ends of his fingers, which had not been covered by the gloves, were dirty and there was no place to wash. "I suppose I'll have to eat whatever slop they give us with these fingers."

Jeff stepped to the door and bowed as the jailer walked in holding a steaming bowl of something grey and lumpy. "Sir, we are wellborn Americans and we wish to send a message to Benjamin Franklin, who will surely reward you for any news concerning us. Will you send this message to him, with this button?"

"Gold!" said the jailer greedily.

"Not at all," said Jeff. "You can tell for yourself it is too light in weight. Weigh it in your hand."

The jailer did so, and spat to one side. "Painted wood! Why do you want to send this?"

"Why, as proof that they are indeed Americans in spite of their aristocratic garb," put in Marcel. "Who but these rustics from the wild western forests would dress up to visit Versailles, yet wear buttons like these. No Austrian or Frenchman would dream of it."

"That's right," said Jeff, relieved at Marcel's coming up with so pat an explanation.

"Jailer," went on Marcel with increased confidence, "in your hand you have proof that these men are undoubtedly Americans and not Viennese spies."

"So what?" said the jailer. "They still stole a diamond necklace and will be executed in a few days if the necklace is not returned. Or even if it is. And what care I? I have my wife Marie and my own children to feed, and I shall not do that long if I spend too much time talking to prisoners."

"On the other hand, you will feed your family better if you carry this message and the button to the good Franklin. Even if these men are to be executed, Franklin would still pay for the privilege of seeing them before they die. He is rich. He may pay you a year's wages. What would that sum be to him?"

"There is that possibility," said the jailer, his grimy fist closing around Jeff's scrap of cotton and the button of a material that did not exist in Franklin's time. "Now eat your nice gruel, you scum, and if this man Franklin does not pay, you spies will have a most miserable time before you die."

Fargo inspected the food after the jailer had gone. "I always did hate hot cereals, especially lumpy ones, but if we're not going to eat again till tomorrow, I suppose we ought to try to get some of it down."

Marcel produced two pieces of wood he had apparently kept as clean as possible. "My friends, here are two plates. Pray divide the food and eat as much as you wish. Since my own execution is nigh, there is no reason for me to weigh myself down needlessly with food."

"You can't tell," said Fargo, his irrepressible optimism

bouncing back in spite of the food and the jailer's threat. "Better eat a good third of it, Marcel. We will persuade the good Benjamin Franklin to buy your freedom, too."

"Impossible, I'm afraid. He might send word to you, but he will not come himself. Jouncing in a carriage is very hard on the old man."

"Even a messenger might be of help."

"Agreed," said Marcel. "A message from Franklin might buy enough time for you to give the authorities a chance of finding the jewels you are supposed to have stolen. But as for me, there will be no time for help. I will be gone, perhaps, before the messenger even arrives. Nevertheless, my friends, I thank you heartily for your intended kindness to me."

All three of them worried down the gruel in silence and drank from the pitcher of stale water that the jailer had also brought.

Fargo said, "I wonder if we'll ever find Albany. I keep telling myself she's a cop, a strong, brave cop who can take care of herself, but I can't bear the thought of losing her somewhere in time."

Jeff said, "I'm sure that wherever she is, she is much safer than we are. And if she's in Versailles and hears about us she might even arrange our release."

Fargo said, "You scribbled something else on that message to Franklin before you gave it to the jailer. Did it have anything to do with Albany?"

"Not quite. It was something else. I wanted him to bring a small lightning rod with him. I thought it might help me reach Norby."

"You mean, like an antenna."

"More or less. I'll snatch at any chance."

They had grown accustomed to speaking in French and were doing so without thought.

Marcel, who had been listening with a look of intense interest on his face, said, "My dear friends, do not be offended if I ask a question. I know well the lightning rod, which, after all, is an invention of your compatriot, Franklin. All the world knows of this and of its miraculous way of fending off the lightning bolt. But who is this Norby you speak of whom you wish to reach? Is it another powerful compatriot?"

"In a way," said Jeff. "Norby is an automaton, like those your family made, but much more advanced. I can give him orders by talking to him, even across a distance."

"You tell me this seriously? You are not amusing yourself at the expense of a poor man who is about to die?" said Marcel earnestly.

"No, no, Marcel. I tell you nothing but the truth. My automaton speaks and reasons and has marvellous abilities."

"Alas, alas. I wish to believe you, but to do so would increase my unhappiness a hundredfold. I would like to see this automaton. If it is indeed as you say, I would give my life to see it—but instead I must give my life before I see it. How sad I am!"

"If we can save your life, Marcel," said Jeff, "then perhaps you will see Norby in time. It all depends on Franklin."

"Ah, the good Franklin. He is a scientist and he is interested in automata, too. He attended one of the last exhibitions given by my father before he died. Yes, he did. Even," (here Marcel paused dramatically) "even His Majesty, Louis the Sixteenth attended and spoke graciously to my father.

His Majesty is a skilled locksmith, you must know. It is indeed a great pity he was born to the kingship, having such a future as a locksmith and mechanic."

Fargo asked, "Does the King know you are in prison?"

"Would that be likely?" said Marcel. "Who would bother to tell him? But you must not concern yourself with me, but with yourselves. Will Monsieur Franklin truly recognize that the false gold button was made in America? He has not been there for many years and he may not know this new invention."

"He'll know that the button wasn't made in Europe," said Jeff. "He's a very intelligent man."

"So he is. There are those who think he is in league with the devil—did you know that? I have heard some ignorant folk say that the lightning rod is a powerful magic and dangerous to use."

Fargo said, "I hope you don't believe that."

"Not at all. My father taught me that every automaton was simply a mechanism that could be understood, even though the onlookers suspected supernatural powers. And with that, I grew firmly convinced that there is no magic. Although your pen that writes without ink is a little hard to understand. And I can't help but wonder at an automaton that responds to spoken commands. Perhaps there is a small person within Norby, someone my size?" Marcel questioned.

"No, no," said Jeff. "There's only machinery inside my Norby. He's much smaller than you are."

"Then if he can move freely, his clockwork must be quite miniscule. Would he be light enough to be lifted by balloon?"

"What kind of balloon?"

"Why, *a* balloon. Surely you have heard of the balloons that have recently risen, carrying people. Some say it will be the next step in transportation! But they are dangerous, I think. They are filled with hydrogen, which can easily go up in flames. Do you have balloons in the nation of the United States?"

Fargo said, "Not yet." Then, suddenly frowning, "I wish I could get into a balloon and rescue Albany. I keep thinking she's in Versailles. After all, that's where the Queen's necklace, the real one, was supposed to go."

Jeff, remembering that Albany had both the replica and the necklace with the real diamonds, wondered how the court would react to Albany's appearing in their midst. He shrugged.

Marcel said, "Careful, my friends. Sometimes these walls have ears, for there are guards who are supposed to listen when we are unwary and talk among ourselves. If you speak of jewels, then you will be beyond help. Even Franklin wouldn't save you if you have actually stolen jewels belonging to the court."

"I assure you, Marcel," said Jeff. "We have stolen no jewels—but we can't explain what really happened. No one would believe us."

He was beginning to wonder if anything might be heard from Franklin. The old man was only a few miles away, but this was 18th-century France. There were no forms of powered transportation. The steam engine had been invented but it had not yet been added to ships or locomotives. Of course, there were no gasoline or nuclear engines, and no one had even imagined the antigrav devices that lifted cars and the hyperdrive that powered spaceships in Jeff's own century. In the France of Louis the Sixteenth, all people who wished to travel over land either walked, rode horses, or rode in vehicles pulled by horses.

Jeff had just decided that no one would come—or that if someone came, it would be too late—when the jailer's big key grated in the lock.

Fargo, never the pessimist, jumped up eagerly. "Franklin?"

But Marcel shook his head. "I fear it is only my impending doom. They have come to lead me to the execution. See—there is the executioner behind the jailer. He wears a black mask, for he does not wish to be recognized. It is a shameful occupation, though of course a most necessary one."

"You mean he's going to do it here?" said Jeff.

"Don't want to get this nice dungeon all bloody, do we?" said the second jailer—he was not the same one who had gone off with the message. He smiled evilly, for he had several teeth missing and looked as if he had fangs. "We take this condemned man out to the executioner's block. The executioner, Petit-Pierre here," (he jerked a thumb at the hulking, massive man behind him) "wants to get a look at the two spies he will take care of tomorrow. He is a most conscientous worker."

"But we are not spies—we're honest Americans," said Jeff desperately.

The jailer shrugged. "Call yourselves what you wish. You will be executed as spies."

Marcel tugged at Jeff's sleeve. "There is no use arguing with the jailer, my friend. Come, let us instead ask him a favor.—Jailer, may these American gentlemen come into the inner courtyard that they may pray for me when I die? Surely you will not deny a dying man a last gift."

The jailer grinned again. "You wish these men who will

29

die tomorrow to watch you die today? Instead of a priest? Why not? You will but go to the kingdom down below the more surely."

Jeff said, "But Marcel, we cannot bear—"

Marcel said, "Please, my friends. You have made my last hours pleasurable with your company. I will die more easily for your continued company. My only regret is that I will never see your automaton, friend Jeff."

The executioner's block was horribly stained with dried blood. Jeff wished he hadn't come, although the cold air helped to clear his mind. If only he could concentrate on Norby, all might yet be well—but all he could think of was poor shivering Marcel ready to march between the armed soldiers lined up before the executioner's block.

For some reason, Marcel was beaming. "I'm to be decapitated," he said. "But that is wonderful."

"Wonderful?" said Jeff with stupefaction.

"Indeed. How proud my father would feel if he knew. Decapitation is for aristocrats. Poor devils like myself are hanged. This is the good King's work. He did not wish a fellow clockmaker to be hanged as though he were scum. He *did* hear about me after all."

Fargo said, "It would be better if he freed you."

Marcel shrugged. "You ask too much. The Austrian Queen and her favorites would never allow it. And they have too much power over the softhearted King."

"Come," growled the jailer. "I'm not here to listen to all this fine talk. I'm a hardworking man and so is Petit-Pierre. Others wait their turn. On your knees before the block, small criminal—"

But at that moment, Jeff heard footsteps pounding

through the courtyard. A plainly-dressed young man ran up to them, accompanied by a puffing fat man to whom the jailer and the executioner bowed respectfully, while the soldiers presented arms.

"I'm Benjamin Franklin's grandson," said the young man in perfect French. He looked from one prisoner to another and then addressed Fargo. "My name is also Benjamin, but I am usually known as Benny. The Lieutenant of the Bastille has permitted me to interview you in order to find out if you are really Americans."

The lieutenant said haughtily, "The United States is an ally of France. If, therefore, you are American citizens, I will place you in the custody of Mr. Franklin. If, however, the jewels are not recovered and it is clear that you participated in the theft, you will be executed—Americans or not. The King's justice is not to be overturned."

"Lieutenant," said Fargo, "we didn't steal anything. My brother and I are the famous Wells brothers, American actors and conjurers. We're in Paris to give a show."

The lieutenant snorted. "Then what were you doing at the Boehmer-Bossange establishment? Practicing levitation on diamonds?"

Fargo bestowed a brilliant smile upon him. "No, Lieutenant. I am sure the jewelers will find that they themselves have merely mislaid whatever it is they claim they have lost. The truth is—"

Jeff held his breath. He himself hated to lie and was so bad at it he had given up trying, but he had to admire Fargo's easy glibness.

"—we wanted to have an early performance today."

"Where, Sir Conjurer?"

31

"In the woods near Le Trianon, hoping to please the Queen."

"In the woods? In the very middle of winter?"

"We American are hardy people and I am of the northern forests. We hoped the Queen would see us from her window."

"And you could see the ladies, no doubt? Are all you Americans like your Franklin?"

"Be more respectful to my grandfather, Lieutenant," said Benny indignantly.

"I assure you, sir," said the lieutenant, leering, "I admire him. His popularity with the ladies, at his age—"

"And so," continued Fargo, "my brother and I were searching for a tailor, without whom we would not be able to perform."

"Why did you need a tailor?"

Silently Fargo turned around and bent over.

It was clear to Jeff that the lieutenant was impressed with the evidence of the need.

Fargo went on. "We inquired about a tailor's shop, and some lout gave us the wrong direction. He told us to bang on the back door, which we did. The door opened and we found Monsieur Boehmer lying on the floor, unconscious. Perhaps he had been robbed, but not by us. When he woke, he accused *us* of theft."

Marcel said, "That sounds convincing."

The lieutenant cast a look of disapproval at him. "Not convincing. Merely suggestive. You must convince me that you are genuinely American. Your accent is odd."

Benny interposed. "These gentlemen knew my grandfather's words to the signers of the Declaration of Independence about hanging together or hanging separately—but perhaps we need additional evidence. Can you speak English as well as write it?"

Fargo cleared his throat. " 'When in the course of human events, it becomes necessary for one people to dissolve the political bands which have connected them with another . . .' "

Fargo's resonant tenor went on, speaking English with only a slight Terran accent. " 'We hold these truths to be self-evident, that all men are created equal, that they are endowed by their Creator with certain unalienable rights, that among these are life, liberty, and the pursuit of happiness . . .' "

"Excellent," said Benny, "although your accent is a trifle odd. Are you from one of the wilder western territories?"

"Sort of," said Fargo, "but we are definitely Americans."

"And reciting revolutionary and seditious nonsense," muttered the lieutenant. "I understand enough English to know *that*."

"It was the American Declaration of Independence, Lieutenant, an independence your gracious king was pleased to help us achieve," said Benny. He turned to Fargo. "My grandfather was intrigued by your button and wishes to discuss it with you, but he was puzzled by your request for a lightning rod."

"Did you bring one?" asked Jeff, trying to stand between Marcel and the lieutenant and afraid each instant that the latter would suddenly order the execution to proceed.

"In this old sword-stick," said Benny, unscrewing the head of a cane he had brought. "I assure you, Lieutenant, that there's no sword in here. May I bring out the lightning rod?"

"Let him," said the executioner in a hoarse voice. "I have

always wanted to see a lightning rod up close. They say they are made in the devil's workshop."

Benny took out the small lightning rod and put it in Jeff's outstretched hand.

Petit-Paul muttered, "It is only an iron stick. Is that all?" He sounded dreadfully disappointed.

"Thanks," said Jeff, putting both hands around it and closing his eyes.

"Pay no attention to him," said Fargo. "In the chaos of our arrest, we lost our wands. I can do without; I use my hands. My brother, however, insists on a wand, and with it he acts to make an automaton appear—a mere conjurer's trick, of course."

"My grandfather is most interested in automata," said Benny, "and I am quite convinced you are Americans. With the lieutenant's permission, I will take you to Passy to meet my grandfather. Do you have your automaton with you?"

"Let us see," said Fargo. "If my brother's conjuring works properly, he will come to the lightning rod, floating through the air by means of an invisible balloon."

"Incredible," said Benny. "Does it come to the lightning rod because there is a magnetic sympathy?"

The lieutenant became suddenly aware that other business was being neglected. "Get on with this execution," he roared. "Petit-Paul, we do not pay you to play the role of an ugly statue."

Petit-Paul growled deep in his throat and motioned to Marcel. "Your head down on the block, you."

Jeff thought, Please, Norby, tune into me. Then he looked up at the block to see Marcel waving at him.

Having attracted Jeff's attention, Marcel said cheerfully,

"Good-bye, my American friends. I am so happy to have known you."

Jeff dashed up to the block, one hand outstretched and the other still holding the lightning rod. Before the executioner could object, he shook Marcel's hand and was embarrassed when the little prisoner clung to him, kissing him on both cheeks.

It had started to snow a bit earlier and the flakes were now coming down hard and steadily. The flakes melted on Jeff's face and the moisture hid the tears.

"Good-bye, Marcel. I tried—I'm so sorry—"

"Jeff," Marcel cried out excitedly. "Something has appeared over your head. The snow is falling about it. And now—legs—arms—oh, such happiness! It must be your automaton!"

"Norby," yelled Fargo. "Take the little man and Jeff out of here. I'll be with Benjamin Franklin. Marcel, get on Jeff's back."

Every soldier in the place—the executioner, the jailer, the lieutenant—all seemed transfixed, unable to interfere.

"The balloon is really invisible," said Marcel, jumping onto Jeff's back and staring upward. His voice was ecstatic.

"Jeff," asked Norby, "is that man with the axe going to do something I wouldn't like?"

"Right!" Jeff dropped the lightning rod and grabbed Norby's hand as the robot dropped farther down.

Norby said, "Then it's time to leave." And suddenly it wasn't snowing anymore.

4
Time Trouble

Jeff felt woozy. He could see that they had landed in someone's room, but he felt himself to be still floating. He was standing on a faded, worn rug, but it seemed insubstantial beneath his feet. All the massive furniture was carved from dark wood, as were the glass-front bookcases. Floor-to-ceiling glass doors in one wall opened onto a terrace and beyond there was a formal garden in bloom, although Jeff found it difficult to see anything clearly.

"I see everything blurry," said Norby. "Do you?"

"Everything is clear to me except you two," said Marcel. "You two seem faded, as if I can almost see through you." He was standing near a table piled with papers, and he held one up. "Everything in life has suddenly become a puzzle, so I don't mind one more. See, Jeff, this newspaper is in English, I am certain, and the date is April 16, 1896. How is that possible? Can we have moved by some powerful science into the future and into England?"

"I was trying to go home," said Norby, "but I think the necklace brought me here. It's lying on the shelf in that bookcase."

Jeff and Norby looked at the necklace. Except for being dusty, it seemed the same as the replica Albany had worn for the ill-fated skit in Manhattan.

"Please," said Marcel. "Is this travel-in-time the deed of the automation that speaks for itself?"

"I'll try to explain," said Jeff. And in as few words as possible, making use of terms he thought would be understood by a man of the 18th century, he explained about robots and about Norby's abilities. "Can you believe me, Marcel?"

Marcel looked pale. "It is very difficult, my friend. You are from still farther in the future and you make use of advanced science. I try to believe, Jeff, but thinking of it gives me a headache."

"Listen, Jeff," said Norby, "we're in danger, and we can't stay here. I've been trying to tune into our own time. The necklace replica is definitely there, but something is awfully wrong. Ever since I was near it in the museum, I've felt it pull me, but—"

"But if that's the case," said Jeff, trying to focus, "if the replica is home and is pulling you, why don't you just follow the pull and go home, Norby?"

Norby said, "Well, I think history has changed."

Jeff said, "You mean that because history has changed, there's no way we can go home? That we don't exist there in this new history? Maybe the world as we know it doesn't exist? Is that what you are saying?"

"That's what I am saying, Jeff. Starting now in the 18th century, there must be two time-tracks, because something you, Fargo, or Albany did when you entered the 18th century started a new track. Marcel belongs to the past, so he fits into either track and he's here. You and I, Jeff, don't belong at all to one of the tracks. And as far as this track is concerned, this is the farthest forward I can get. And maybe only because the necklace replica is here. Even so we don't fit here and we're fading out."

"Fading out of existence?"

"That's right."

"We can't allow that, Norby. We must go back and correct the mistake that changed history," Jeff said.

"I suppose it was something that stupid Fargo did. He always acts without thinking."

"Wait, Norby. Don't jump to conclusions. It might be something Albany did in Versailles, or wherever she went. And she's wearing the replica that travels in time. Look, Albany was wearing the device, and the jewelers also had it. The two replicas were the same, although in different time periods. One of those two entered history as it was supposed to, for here it is in England. If we take this replica, it might guide us back to the other version of itself. And in that way we'll get either to Albany or the jewelers, depending on which version this is. Then we'll find out what's been happening to change history."

Jeff, totally unconcerned with the fact that he was planning burglary, tried to open the door of the cabinet. His hand went right through it as if there wasn't any piece of furniture there.

"I'm solid," said Marcel. "I could take it out for you."

"No," said Norby. "Don't do it. That's not the answer. We'd just be upsetting this time-track and setting up a total of *three* time-tracks. We have to find the necklace at the point in time where everything was changed. And then we must shift the time-tracks back to what they were. The trouble is, I don't know how we can find it."

"Someone is coming!" said Marcel, pointing to the garden.

A tall, thin man in a tweed suit, carrying a potted geranium plant, ambled through the garden, opened the glass door, and entered the library.

"Bless my soul, a guest!"

"I speak only French, sir," said Marcel with an expressive wave of his hands, "and I apologize for intruding on your privacy. We have come here by mistake."

"That is fine! I speak French, too, as you now see. But you say 'we'. Are there others here?" The man looked about him in a rather confused manner. "I see only you."

"Pardon." Marcel looked down at his shabby, dirty clothes. "I am a French actor, rehearsing for a play about prisoners in the Bastille over a hundred years ago and—"

"Ah, I see, and well-costumed too. Jolly good thing, I've often thought, that they tore down the Bastille during the French Revolution—"

"They did? There was a revolution?" Marcel sat down abruptly in a chair.

"In 1789. How can you not remember? July 14 is the French national holiday, the anniversary of the fall of the Bastille."

"Yes, of course," said Marcel. "I have periods of forgetfulness." He passed his hand over his forehead and said, "Do not be alarmed sir. I am not a dangerous lunatic. I have never harmed anyone in my life. Still, I sometimes think I hear voices and see visions. A harmless peculiarity."

The Englishman laughed. "Oh, well, we have our eccentrics in this country as well, and the English have long known that the French are capable of anything."

He pulled at a bell rope hanging near the cabinet and sat down. "I have rung for tea. Please remain seated. You look hungry and in need of something to eat to restore your mental clarity. If you need a bath, I can supply that, but I don't think I have clothes that would fit you."

"Pray do not discommode yourself," said Marcel. "I thank you for your hospitality. Something to eat and drink is all I need and then I will leave."

Jeff whispered, "Ask him how he got the necklace and what he's going to do with it."

"Remarkable," said the Englishman. "Are you a ventriloquist? Your lips did not move but I thought I could hear faint sounds, almost like words, coming from a few feet to your left."

"Your pardon, sir. I make these mistakes. But tell me about some of the things here. I could not help but notice the necklace in your cabinet. It resembles pictures of one that was famous in France."

"The Queen's necklace," said the gentleman, smiling. "You might wonder why I leave it in an unlocked cabinet for anyone to take who wanders in as you did—"

"Oh, sir—"

"I am not accusing you. But the necklace is a worthless duplicate, and is only there as a curio. It was brought to England after the French Revolution."

"As I recall, the real diamonds were stolen and blame for the affair fell upon the Queen," said Marcel, repeating the words Jeff had whispered in his ear.

"So it was. I know the story well. The jewelers thought Cardinal Rohan was buying the necklace on the Queen's orders. They took it to him on the first of February in 1785. That same day, Rohan handed it to the Countess de la Motte, who gave it to a man she said was the Queen's messenger. Rohan received a paper in return, supposedly signed by the Queen."

"But it was not the Queen's messenger?" asked Marcel, his eyes alight with interest.

The tea arrived and Marcel's eyes widened even more, for it was a lavish high tea, deposited by a little parlor maid who curtseyed and looked, with distinct disapproval, at the small guest with the dirty face and dirty clothes. She curtseyed again and left as the Englishman poured out tea and urged cakes, sandwiches, and scrambled eggs on the starving Frenchman.

"The messenger was a man working for the thief, La Motte," continued the Englishman, while Jeff's mouth watered for food he couldn't pick up, much less taste. "He was conspiring with his wife to steal the necklace. She was ultimately caught, branded, and whipped. When she escaped later to England, she wrote an article vilifying Marie Antoinette. Eventually, most Frenchmen believed that their foreign queen had indeed tried to buy the necklace secretly and had used La Motte as a scapegoat. Not true, of course, but when everyone believes a lie, it might as well be the truth."

"Marcel," said Jeff, "ask him if he thinks the affair of the Queen's necklace brought about the Revolution."

"Odd," said the Englishman, "but it has just fallen into my head that there is some question about whether the affair of the Queen's necklace caused the Revolution. Certainly, Napoleon said he thought so. And certainly it brought the Queen into such unpopularity that it was impossible for the royal family to ride out the Revolution. They were inevitably beheaded."

41

Marcel nodded calmly, even though he must have been profoundly shocked at the statement that the King and Queen lost their lives in violent insurrections.

When tea was over at last Marcel rose and bowed courteously. "Your hospitality has been superb, sir," he said. "I am deeply honored and immensely grateful. My mind feels much clearer. Before leaving might I ask what you plan to do with the replica you have."

"Why, nothing at all. It will simply sit in my cabinet."

"Very well. I must find my way back to the rest of my troupe. Thank you once again, and if ever you need the help of Marcel Oslair, you may count on it in full measure." And he bowed again.

The Englishman bowed, too. "Glad to have been of help. If you are ever in the neighborhood again, Monsieur Oslair, please return and we can talk again of the Queen's necklace. It is an interesting story."

Marcel paused in the doorway to the garden. "Sir, do you believe in marvellous things to come?"

"Why not? I have read 'The Time Machine', the new novel by Mr. Herbert George Wells, and it struck me that I would like to go into the future and see what is to come."

"Perhaps I shall," said Marcel, smiling shyly. "They say the mad are not bound to one time and place."

"Possibly, but I must get back to my work. Cheerio!"

Marcel opened the glass doors and walked out into the sunlight of the garden. Norby and Jeff sailed past him.

"Come to that grove of trees, Marcel," said Jeff. "We'll try time-travelling from there. Then no one will see you vanish."

Marcel walked out into the colorful summer garden. It had

been winter in France just an hour earlier, but it seemed summer now in England. He said, "I am reluctant to leave this pleasant place."

Norby seized his hand and pulled him toward the woods. "Too bad, Marcel," he said sharply, "but perhaps you don't notice that Jeff is growing fainter and fainter. Do you want him to disappear forever, to vanish out of existence?"

Marcel slapped his forehead in dismay. "I am a villain. I have utterly forgotten." He ran along ahead of them into the cool dimness of the wood.

"Jeff," he said, "my profoundest regrets, good friend. I shouldn't have had tea. It endangered your life."

"No, I wanted you to eat, and I wanted you to ask about the necklace." Jeff could now see nothing but a faint and colorless outline of the landscape around him.

Norby was fading, too, but less so. Part of him was of alien manufacture and appeared stable in this time-track.

"Hurry, Norby," said Jeff. "Take me back to somewhere before the time-tracks diverged. I don't want to fade out completely."

5
Back-Where?

"It's so dark I can't see you, Jeff," said Marcel in alarm. "Have you faded out? Say something, Jeff."

"I'm here," said Jeff loudly.

The darkness was pierced as the beam of light from Norby's hat flashed out. The little robot said, "Good! I can see you. How do you feel?"

"Starving, but not faded," said Jeff, running his hands over the rock in front of him. "My feet can feel the ground and my hands can feel the rock, so wherever or whenever we are, I'm okay. We're now in part of the time-track that includes me, or that *will* include me in the future."

"We're in a cave," said Marcel, "and I think there is something on the walls."

Norby played his light over the wall and Jeff whistled. It was covered with cave paintings of brightly-colored animals that seemed vividly alive. Jeff found himself expecting them to move.

"These are prehistoric paintings," he said. "Perhaps they're freshly painted. How far back in time have we come?"

Marcel said, "Not quite freshly painted. There is dust everywhere and no footprints. Norby, my clever automaton, there's something over there—shine your light."

The three time-travellers looked at the strange object revealed by the light and, for a while, sheer surprise struck then into silence. It was a large bas-relief of an animal shaped in clay on the cave floor, but it was what was *on* the animal that surprised them.

"It's a European bison," said Jeff, "and that's the Queen's necklace laid on its neck. Or at least the replica, without the diamonds. It's not silver; it's that dark metal."

"And it's covered with dust," said Norby. "Marcel is right. If we're in France, as I think we are, then we've arrived here before modern Frenchmen discovered this cave. The carving and the necklace have been here a long time—maybe a *very* long time. I wonder why the replica draws me to the place where it exists: The metal of the necklace must be doing it because there are no fake diamonds here."

"But Albany's missing," said Jeff. "This can't be where she went. When she disappeared she was wearing the replica the way it looked after Boehmer and Bossange turned it into a model for the Queen's necklace by sticking the fake diamonds into it. Do you suppose they found the replica first and modelled the real necklace after it?"

"It does not seem to me there's any way to tell," said Marcel.

"Anyway," said Jeff, "that's not the point right now. We must find Albany and rescue Fargo."

"*And* restore our own time-track of history," said Norby. "That's a big job, Jeff. How is it to be done?"

Marcel said, "We rely on you, Norby. I must no longer think of you as an automaton. It is most clear, my marvelous one, that you are a *person* in your own right, with a mind as good as any other mind."

"As good as?" said Norby indignantly. "I have a better mind than anyone I have ever met. It's even better than Jeff's, isn't it, Jeff?"

"It can certainly do more than mine can," said Jeff cautiously.

"And of course I'm a real person," Norby continued. "I have a special brain constructed by a robot from another planet; one of the Mentor robots made by the Others. When the ship I was on struck an asteroid, I was found by an old Terran spacer named MacGillicuddy—"

"What is a Terran spacer?" asked Marcel.

Jeff said "It's a man from Earth who travels in a ship beyond the atmosphere, in the empty space between the planets."

"To the moon? As in the book by my compatriot, Cyrano de Bergerac?"

"And beyond," said Jeff.

"And the Mentor robots are still more clever automatons, more clever than Norby?"

"Yes."

"And these Mentors were made by the Others?" Marcel shook his head. "Who are the Others?" he asked. "You breathe the word with reverence."

"They are living organisms," said Jeff, "who look a little like human beings, but are a much older race from a world very far away. We met then once in the distant past before they started their advanced civilization, and I would like to meet them again someday."

"You tell me marvels," said Marcel. "What a world you must have in your time."

"The marvels don't do me any good," sighed Jeff. "I'm so hungry—and thirsty."

"There's water dropping from that bit of rock on the ceiling," said Norby.

Jeff went to it and accumulated several mouthfuls. It had a funny taste but was reasonably fresh. And at the moment, that was all he cared about.

"I've brought a sandwich from 1896," said Marcel. "I thought perhaps you would be able to eat it in some other time. I'm sorry, but it's a little dirty from my pocket."

Jeff reached for it eagerly. "Wonderful! I can *feel* it." He devoured it in three bites and licked his lips. "Delicious, but I don't understand why what wasn't real for me in 1896 should be real for me now. I don't understand the paradoxes of time-travel."

"I don't like them at all," said Norby. "I don't like not being able to move through space and time as I wish. I keep being dragged here and there by the replica necklace, and I'm blocked off by wrong time-tracks and—and I just don't like it. I feel like a failure!"

Marcel said to Jeff, "It is the final proof that this wonderful little automaton is not an automaton. He has feelings. Are all the automata of your time like this?"

"Norby is the only one like himself in my time."

"That's because I have important emotive circuits," said Norby. "I'm one of a kind, I am." Then his head lowered into his barrel until only the upper third portion of his eyes was visible. "But I'm one of an inferior kind. I'm a failure."

"You are not," said Jeff. "You're doing your best, and you've done a great deal. You saved Marcel from being executed and you saved me from fading away. I'm sure you'll find Albany and Fargo sooner or later, and we'll straighten out this mess with time, too."

"You can't survive on a sandwich," said Norby morosely.

"You're a human being and need food. And if we try to get some in the past you might change history."

"We've time-travelled before without causing trouble," said Jeff. "I don't think just anything starts a new time-track. It has to be comething crucial like whatever it was Albany, or maybe Fargo, did. I'll bet Marcel's having tea in 1896 didn't change anything."

"My good friends," said Marcel seriously. "It may be that the entire problem, the reason why there is a new time-track, and why you can't go back to your own century, is that I didn't die when I was supposed to. After all, history had changed before I ate the food given me by that hospitable gentleman, who did not mind my intrusion and my dirty face. It would be best if you took me back to my own time in 1785 and let Petit-Pierre, the executioner, do his duty."

Jeff hesitated. That might be the correct explanation. Then he said, "No, that can't be it. I will not have you killed, Marcel."

Marcel's eyes filled with tears. "What a friend you are, Jeff. I do not deserve you."

"Besides," said Jeff, "I have an idea. Listen. Albany vanished with the replica around her neck *before* an earlier version of that same replica could get to her. The result is that the replica exists both in the earlier and later time and goes down through history as it should. We have proof of that because we saw it in the glass cabinet a hundred years later. But the *real* necklace vanished too soon."

"I'm getting mixed up," said Norby.

"The real diamond necklace was on the floor of Boehmer's room and Albany picked it up. That meant the necklace never got to La Motte; it didn't go to England; it wasn't broken up and the diamonds sold. It remained in history intact and the Queen wasn't implicated in any scandal. And maybe she didn't become unpopular enough to be beheaded. Would that change history?"

"But I don't understand any of this," said Marcel. "I cannot comprehend all this talk about revolution."

"I'd explain," said Jeff, "but now that I've had a little bit to eat and drink, I've become so sleepy I can't stand it. I haven't slept since I left Manhattan. Norby, you explain."

"Certainly," said Norby. "I'll ladle some French history into his brain and some Terran Basic, too. He'll need it if he stays with us."

"But can I stay with you? Ought I not be in my own time?"

"Not quite your own time," said Jeff, yawning. "Not if it means your execution. You'll either stay with us or we'll find some safe time for you."

Marcel sat down near Norby. "Since I am given life when I should have been killed, I cannot complain about the terms on which the gift is presented. Come, teach away, my charming little automaton."

Norby was shaking Jeff. "Wake up! Someone's entering the cave."

Jeff woke at once. "Is there somewhere we can hide?"

"Behind that big rock—if nobody looks there."

"Should we leave?" whispered Marcel. He spoke Terran Basic now, thanks to Norby's mind teaching.

"We can't," said Norby. "The necklace is holding us here, and I can't seem to break the bond. I'm *such* a failure."

The three had now moved behind a large rock. Flickering light came closer and closer until two people entered the cave, a young man and a pretty girl. The man was wearing a tunic that stopped short of his knees, and his feet were in stout, leather sandals. A leather belt around his waist bore the scabbard of a long dagger. He carried a torch and wedged it tightly between two stones so that his hands were free.

The girl wore a thin, leather dress with patterns on it, and she carried a dark, woolen cape that she spread on the cave floor. She turned to the young man and held out her arms. She spoke in a lovely, musical voice, and her words sounded slightly familiar to Jeff, but made no sense to him.

"Latin," whispered Marcel in Jeff's ear. "They are Romans. This is the province of Gaul that later became France. She says she's glad they found the cave because it is so well-hidden that on one will disturb them."

Jeff nodded vigorously and put his fingers on Marcel's mouth to make him stop speaking.

The young man kissed the young woman and ran his fingers through her long, reddish hair. Then he looked into the shadows of the cave and cried out, pointing to the wall. The girl jumped up and looked, too, holding her arms up with a cry of wonder and admiration.

They were staring at the paintings on the wall. Forgetting about kisses, the young man picked up his torch and studied the paintings closely. They found the bison form and the girl picked up the necklace, blowing off the dust.

The boy took a leather thong from his belt and pulled it through the metal loops at the back of the necklace where the two long tassels hung down. Laughing, he tied it around the girl's neck and they embraced, talking softly.

Jeff's lips tightened as it occurred to him that if they had used sensible leather thongs on the necklace back in Manhattan, instead of slippery ribbons, none of this would have happened.

Marcel whispered, "They say that the necklace is a gift from the gods to honor their love, and they will keep it forever so that they will love forever. Oh—"

"What's the matter?" asked Jeff.

"It's the dust," he said, gasping. "I'm going to sneeze."

"No!"

The sneeze reverberated through the cave and the young man drew his dagger. He pushed the frightened girl behind him and swaggered toward the big rock. In a tone of bravado he said, "Quid nunc?"

Marcel stood up and held up his right hand. "Salve!"

Jeff stood up too. "Marcel, tell your Roman friend that this cave is sacred to an old religion and we are its caretakers. Tell them they must not enter it again nor tell anyone about it, and they may then have the necklace as a reward. —It's true enough," he muttered to Norby. "With these paintings, it must have been sacred to prehistoric men. I'm not lying."

Marcel spoke to the young Roman couple, who backed away, trembling. And then Norby shot up from behind the rock with a wild screech. The sight of what seemed an undoubted demon was more than the couple could withstand. They ran.

"Vade in pace!" called Marcel after them.

"Now that the necklace has left the cave, Norby," Jeff said, "maybe you can manage some time-travel. Let's get out of here."

He and Marcel each held one of the Norby's hands.

"Find Albany," said Jeff.

The walls of the cave shimmered and shook, but the trio did not vanish.

6
Lost!

"I was hoping we would be in the open air," said Marcel, looking about him despondently in the light of Norby's flash.

"I'm afraid we're still in the cave," said Jeff.

"But, Jeff," said Norby. "I'm certain that I moved."

"You did," said Jeff, "but not in space. Look at the walls—no paintings at all."

"And there's no shaped animal on the cave floor," said Marcel, "only a pile of rocks that must have been placed there deliberately. They couldn't have fallen that way from the roof of the cave."

"The necklace is here. I sense it. The Roman kids took the cave replica away, so that must mean Albany is here with the necklace replica of *our* time," said Norby stubbornly. "It stands to reason. I tuned into the replica, so I had to go where it was."

"Well," said Jeff, "to have moved into the same time as Albany, you would have had to go to 1785 again and there would be *some* signs of the paintings and the carvings. And there'd also be some sign of Albany, and I certainly don't see her. What we've done is move even farther into the past to a time before the carving or the paintings were made, and before the necklace replica was taken away. So it's still here.

It pulled you here, Norby, so you must be able to sense it. Please try."

"Well," said Norby reluctantly, "I sense it's under that pile of rocks.—I guess I'm the world's *record* failure."

"Don't be overdramatic, Norby. Can you get it for us?"

"I think we had better not try," said Marcel. "We are going to have more visitors. This seems to be a rendezvous for lovers through all the ages."

But it wasn't a pair of lovers who came trooping into the cave. As Jeff watched again from behind the rock (it hadn't changed noticeably with time), he saw the lights of many torches casting huge moving shadows over the roof and walls of the cave.

People entered the main chamber in silence, led by a very tall old man wearing a headdress that bore the horns of a bull fastened to the leather. He carried a wooden staff, but no torch, and when he came to the center of the chamber near the pile of rocks, he banged the staff three times on the floor and shouted something in a language Jeff had never heard.

All the people, men and women, wore leather and fur garments. They were all tall and muscular. They positioned their torches in crevices near the largest wall. Two of the women had bundles of twigs they used to brush off the surface of the wall while the others mixed powders in wooden bowls with grease from a leather bag.

The leader dipped his forefinger into one of the bowls and quickly began the outline of a horse on the prepared wall. When the paint ran out, he dipped his finger again and continued until the outline was complete.

Another man took powder from a small bowl and carefully

blew at the horse, creating a dark red area of pigment that he spread into the space within the outline, using a twig that was frayed at one end. Still another, this time a woman, stepped forward and, with a darker paint and a pointed stick, drew fine lines to make a mane for the horse.

When it was done, the leader bowed to the horse and shouted something that sounded musical. The others answered with a rising cadence of tonal notes that died away in echoes. The leader nodded and walked out of the cave while the rest of the group began smiling and talking animatedly as they painted animals on other parts of the wall.

Jeff forgot his hunger while he watched the artists at work. Surely, these must be Cro-Magnon men and women from the Old Stone Age—Paleolithic times.

They painted only a small part of the wall—the whole must have been done over a long period of time—but they finished a number of the animals and seemed happy with their work.

One of them stepped back to admire his work and tripped on the pile of rocks. Jeff alost broke out laughing at the very modern expression of annoyance that swept over the face of the tripper, as well as at the forceful guttural words that went with it. He froze into immobility, however, when the man began heaving rocks from the pile into a dark corner of the cave. What if he should start throwing them behind the big rock?

But suddenly the man uttered a startled exclamation and bent over the pile, moving the rocks aside carefully. A few of the artists stopped to help him, apparently in response to something he said. What they uncovered was a skeleton with long legs laid straight, as if buried there deliberately.

This was no victim of a rockfall. The Cro-Magnon people had stumbled upon a burial site.

Jeff couldn't see the skeleton clearly with so many Cro-Magnon people crowding around, but he could hear their excitement. One of the women screamed as if she had seen something that frightened her, and a man ran out of the cave, returning shortly with the leader.

The old man bent down and picked up something that he held in the torchlight to examine.

"The replica!" whispered Marcel.

"Yes," said Norby.

"Sh," said Jeff, trying to remember what Cro-Magnon people did with unwanted prisoners. Was the skeleton the remains of a human sacrifice? Then he had a worse thought.

Had the necklace replica taken Albany back in time to the Cro-Magnon cave in response to some careless wish or impulse of hers? Suppose the skeleton were Albany's.

Norby was crowding close for a better view, his hand on Jeff's shoulder. He must have caught Jeff's thought, for he responded at once telepathically.

——I don't know whether it's Albany or not. I can't see enough of the skeleton. It's got long legs. Albany is tall. . . .

——No, no, Norby. If it were Albany, it would have the necklace replica as she had it, with the stones in it, not just the black metal as we saw it in Roman times.

——The stones might have been forced off the replica by whoever captured Albany. It might have happened a long time before this.

——. Norby, you're getting me very upset. We don't even know if the skeleton is that of a woman. It might be a man.

——It was *your* thought about Albany.

Norby withdrew into his barrel, his feelings hurt, and Jeff watched with Marcel as the people finished removing the rocks and gathering up the bones of the skeleton. Three of the artists began carrying clay to the site of the burial, shaping it into the rough form of a bison, while the others dug a shallow pit near the entrance to the cave chamber. They placed the bones in it, and over them a pile of wood.

When the bison was shaped, the leader placed the metal of the necklace replica on the animal's neck, stood back, and began chanting. The rest of the people took up the chant and put the flaming ends of several torches to the pile of wood where the skeleton had been placed.

Flames shot up and heavy smoke began to fill the air. Chanting, the people marched out of the cave behind their leader, their voices dying away until there was only the loud, crackling sound of wood burning.

"Norby, get us out of here or we'll suffocate!" said Jeff.

"We could run outside," said Marcel.

"Outside is the primitive world of the ice ages, with only primitive cavemen for company. We are perhaps thirty thousand years in the past."

Jeff's statement seemed to frighten Norby. "We're lost here, Jeff," he wailed. "Lost in the far past! I want to go home, and I can't. I'm a failure. I'm a failure."

"Stop it," said Jeff forcefully. "We're not lost and there's no use wanting to go home now. We don't exist there. We've got to find Albany, and we've got to go where the necklace took her so we can stop whatever formed the new time-track."

"But how are we going to find Albany?" asked Norby. "Maybe all there is of her is that skeleton."

Jeff shivered. "I don't believe it. But even if it is true, then

56

we must go farther back to where she's still alive and save her."

"Maybe we can't," said Norby. "Maybe what killed her will kill us, too."

Marcel said, between coughs, "Maybe she wasn't killed. Maybe she became some caveman's wife and just died naturally. Maybe that was far in the past of even this time, and she died of old age."

Jeff was coughing, too. "We can't sit here coughing and maybeing. Climb on my back again, Marcel. It's a good thing you're small enough to fit into Norby's personal field with me. Get us out of here at once, Norby."

Norby grabbed Jeff's hand and there was a terrible lurch.

"Well, we're not in the cave any longer," said Marcel with some relief in his voice. "I was very tired of the cave. And it's warmer, too."

Norby's light revealed a large room filled with display cases. The floor was cream-colored marble and the ceiling was a pleasant coral pink festooned with hanging chandeliers that seemed to be in all colors, from all periods of human interior decoration. Inside the cases were a multitude of objects, all used to decorate human homes or bodies.

"It's a museum!" said Jeff. "But I certainly don't think it's part of the Metropolitan in Manhattan."

"Those must be windows," said Marcel. "I don't see how we can light the candles in the chandeliers, but perhaps when it is daylight, light will flood the room from outside. Then we can see everything without Norby's smokeless torch."

"Norby's smokeless torch is an electric-powered light, and those chandeliers are electric-powered, too—at least when they're lit up," said Jeff. "Someday I'll explain it to you."

57

"So much to learn," murmured Marcel in a kind of sad excitement.

"And it may not be nighttime. The windows may simply be polarized into opacity."

"What does that mean, my friend?" said Marcel, obviously confused.

"It will have to be explained, too, someday. Is the necklace here, Norby?"

"Yes, in this case," said Norby, his voice rather low and hard to hear. "But I suppose I've made a mistake."

Marcel said, "If the windows are pol—polarated—is there any way of unpolarating them?"

"Polarized," said Norby. "I'll do it." He zoomed over to the window and found the right control. Gradually the window cleared and light entered the room. The scene outside could be seen clearly, bathed in brilliant sunlight.

"Ah, how beautiful," said Marcel. "This must be one of the best gardens on earth."

Jeff had been staring at the necklace, which looked exactly as he had seen it in the cave, minus the fake diamonds that had been in it when it was around Albany's neck. Could Albany have been here? Then he turned to look out the window.

It was indeed a magnificent garden, and one that could be used, for there were small children on swings, and others running around a lily pond playing with golden balls. But he noted that not all the children were human.

Marcel must have noticed, too, for he stepped back from the window in sudden fright. "Look," he said, "demons!"

"No, no," said Jeff. "Just aliens from other planets, I suspect."

58

"Is this the way things are in your time, Jeff? Demons, or aliens, playing with human children?"

"No, not quite. Earth contains only human beings even in my time. But my brother and I have been taken by Norby to other worlds where we have seen aliens. None of the aliens I see here are familiar to me except—there—see that pair of small dragons? They're from a planet called Jamya, one of my most favorite places. I'm glad that in the future, our future, human and alien beings are happy together. This is our future, isn't it, Norby?"

The little robot had gone back to stare at the necklace.

"Norby! What's wrong?"

"I don't know why I transported us here, Jeff. It doesn't make sense. I thought I was tuning into something, but I couldn't have been, unless—"

"Unless what?"

"Unless it hasn't happened yet."

"What are you talking about, Norby? You tuned into the necklace and there it is. It isn't your fault Albany isn't here."

"But that's not the necklace, Jeff. That's a fake."

"Of course it's a fake, if you're thinking of the Queen's necklace with the diamonds. This is only a replica, and it's just the metal—not even the fake diamonds."

"No, Jeff. I mean it's a fake replica. It's not the dark metal that the replica should be made of. It's just a plastic model of the replica. It's a replica of the replica."

"But that's not possible."

"It has to be possible because it's so. I'm sorry, Jeff. It's probably my fault. I guess I'm still just a mixed-up robot. I don't know where we are. We are really, *really* lost."

"Really, *really* lost," echoed Marcel in dismay.

"Yes. I don't know if we're in the past or the future. I don't even know what planet we're on?"

"Isn't this earth?" asked Jeff in astonishment.

"I wish it were," said Norby, "but my sensors tell me the gravity of this planet is different from that of Earth. Not much, but some—enough to tell me that we are not on Earth. But where we are, where in the whole Universe, I don't know. It seems that every step we take moves us farther away from Albany, from Fargo, and from any chance of undoing this mess we've made of time. I'm the worse failure in the whole *Universe.*"

7
Albany

Jeff tried to be calm. "Norby," he said, "you mustn't let your emotive circuits get the better of you. You and I have been in strange places before and we've been lost before. Marcel, please don't be frightened. We will find a way out of this."

"I am not frightened, my friend," said the little Frenchman, walking back to the window. "If we are lost on a strange planet that has happy children and beautiful flowers, then I am content. It is an improvement on the Bastille and on the ugly Petit-Pierre, is it not?"

Jeff and Norby joined him at the window.

"Yes," said Jeff, "a great improvement. What a pity we can't stay. We must find Albany somehow. If that was her skeleton in the cave, we must find her in time before she dies and is buried. We must also go back to your time, Marcel, to rescue Fargo and try to straighten out the time paradoxes. Once we re-establish the proper time-track, we will be able to go home at last."

"I hope you will succeed," said Marcel, "but that is a great deal to do."

Marcel and Jeff were looking at each other seriously, but Norby had continued to stare at the garden. Suddenly he cried out, "It's disappeared."

"What!" said Jeff, looking up.

"The garden," Norby said. "It was there one moment, filled with children of various species—and now it's gone."

In place of the garden was a flat concrete pavement leading to low white buildings. Between them, Jeff could see a landscape of low, treeless hills. There was no vegetation anywhere unless the patches of darkness on the hills were small shrubs.

"Jeff, what happened?" It was Albany's voice.

Jeff and Marcel turned—Norby didn't have to since he had eyes on both sides of his head—and there was Albany in her Marie Antoinette costume, the replica necklace tied around her neck and the true diamond necklace in her hand.

The room had changed, too. It was smaller and dials and switches appeared on the walls in place of the display cabinets that had been there earlier. The ceiling was grey like the walls and the floor.

"I don't remember your being near me in the jeweler's shop," said Albany. "How did you come along? And why do you look as if you'd been in a fight? Where's Fargo, when did Norby arrive, and who is this other man?"

"Albany, did you just this minute come from that room we landed in when we left the museum stage?" asked Jeff.

"Yes. Don't you remember? Boehmer's room, with that other replica snaking toward me? I just wished that I were anywhere else and, wham! Suddenly, I'm here and so are you. And how did you get here, Norby? For that matter, where *is* here?" She looked about, puzzled.

"I wish I knew," said Norby.

Marcel bowed to Albany. "I am pleased to meet the

62

Albany Jones we have been searching for. We thought, earlier in the cave—"

Jeff anxiously signalled him to be quiet. The possible death and burial of Albany in a cave in prehistoric Earth was something they had to make sure wouldn't happen. And, meanwhile, there was no need to refer to it. Albany mustn't know, Jeff felt.

"Let me introduce Marcel Oslair," said Jeff. "We've had some adventures in time over a period of a couple of days while you were moving—wham—from Boehmer to here." Briefly, he told of the Bastille, the Englishman, and the cave. He mentioned the bones but omitted the possibility that they were Albany's.

Albany was too intelligent to miss the possibility, however. "If the metal of the replica was on the bones," she said, touching the replica she was wearing, "then the bones might have been mine, mightn't they?"

"Well—," said Jeff, looking miserable.

"Don't mope about it, Jeff. If they're mine, they're mine. That's my future, but the future isn't written in stone. Those bones may be part of the wrong time-track you spoke of. If we get back to the right time-track, I won't die on prehistoric Earth but in some other place and at some other time."

"Albany's right, Jeff," said Norby. "That's the whole point—the right and wrong time-tracks. There's one that leads to our history, to us and the skit in the museum; and there's another track that changes history into something in which we don't exist. Don't you see?"

Jeff looked blank and Albany said, "Well, I don't. What are you getting at, Norby?"

"Suppose it was the fact that Albany took the necklace back into prehistoric times that changed history, that formed the new time-track. In that case, history would have changed the instant Albany left Boehmer's room. You and I, Jeff—and Fargo, too—would all have begun to fade. But we didn't. We stayed perfectly solid all through the time in the Bastille. We only began to fade when we moved into the future."

"Well, then," asked Albany, "what *did* change history?"

"Something that must have happened in 1785," said Norby, "maybe just after we left the Bastille. We'll have to go back to 1785, find out what it was, and change it back."

"I think you're right, Norby," Jeff said. "In our time-track, the King and Queen of France were executed and France became a republic for a while. If the affair of the Queen's necklace had never happened, Marie Antoinette wouldn't have been blamed for it. Maybe there would never have been a Revolution."

"I wonder," said Marcel thoughtfully. "There was much revolutionary sentiment in France, and there was no love for the Queen, although she became more mature and less frivolous after the birth of the Dauphin."

"The Dauphin died in 1789, just before the Revolution," said Norby.

"Poor child," said Marcel. "Then the King's brother would succeed."

"No," said Jeff. "There was another son, wasn't there, Norby?"

"That's right," said Norby. "It's in my memory banks. On March 27, 1785, less than two months after the necklace was stolen by La Motte—on our time-track—the Queen had a second son. He was Louis the Seventeenth, after his father was beheaded. He wasn't crowned, of course, because the Revolution had taken place. And eventually he disappeared—"

Jeff said, "Yes, but even it the Revolution took place, it might have been less violent. Suppose the people hadn't hated Marie Antoinette enough to kill her and keep her son from the throne. What would have happened?"

"They established a constitutional monarchy for a while. Like in England," said Norby. "Maybe that would have stayed."

Albany said, "That would have been nice. No Reign of Terror. But how could that have changed history so much?"

"Yes, and so much that we wouldn't exist in our own century?" said Jeff.

All four of them stood silent and puzzled until Albany untied the replica and then tied the real diamonds around her neck. "Fargo is lost in France," she said. "The Revolution is only four years away. We're here—somewhere, sometime—in a strange world and a strange situation that perhaps was not meant to be. And all of this was caused by our actions. Is it my fault, I wonder?"

"No," said Jeff. "I'm the one that tied the back tassels of the replica."

"You didn't know what would happen. How could you?" said Albany.

"Norby was telling me not to," said Jeff.

Albany ruffled his hair and said, "You still couldn't know. Perhaps it's no one's fault. We just fell into a situation we couldn't foresee. But you know, Jeff, those bones you saw *could* have been mine. Perhaps it will be necessary for me to die in order to put history right. I don't want to, but if it's necessary, I'll be ready for it."

"Somebody's coming," said Norby. "Somebody heavy."

No one had thought to go out the room's door to see what was on the other side, and now it slid open to admit a huge robot with three eyes and two sets of arms.

"Aliens!" it said, in a low, surprised voice. Then, loudly, "What are you doing here?"

Marcel said, "What language is that, Jeff? Do you understand it?"

"It's the language of the Others," said Jeff in awe. "I do understand it. This is a robot similar to those who made the part of Norby that's extraterrestrial." Switching to Jamyn, Jeff asked, "Where are we, sir?"

"You are in the museum section of the main computer center of this planet. Ah, I now see how you four have arrived without being detected." The robot stepped in front of Albany, towering over her. "This life-form has two disguised versions of a forbidden travel device. The one around the neck is not operational, but the one held in the hand is. It is illegal for you to be in possession of it." The robot held out one of its hands as though expecting Albany to place the replica in it.

Albany did not do so. She backed away. "How do you know about these devices?"

"Are you surprised at our knowledge? Look!" The robot touched a wall switch and a panel slid back to reveal a lighted cubicle containing another dark-metal, no-diamond necklace.

"It's the same model of the replica that we saw before the room changed," said Norby in French.

"Do not speak an alien language!" said the large robot. "Visitors to the museum are supposed to arrive in the transporter chamber in the proper way, with proper credentials and with funds for the tickets. No matter what language visitors speak among themselves, they must speak Galactic to us and to other visitors of a different species. How is it you don't know these elementary facts? Where are you from?"

"We are from the planet Earth," said Jeff.

"There is no such planet. It is not listed as belonging to the Galactic Federation."

While Albany whispered to a puzzled Marcel what it was that the robot was saying, Norby said, "Jeff, I think we'd better tell this inferior Mentor robot the truth. It's just possible he might be able to help us."

Jeff nodded. "I think you're right.—Sir, we are lost in time. The time-travel device brought us here—"

"It is a space-travel device," said the robot. "It brings about time-travel because it is defective. That is why it should not be used. There should be no such device in existence—only this model in the museum."

"But such a device reached us and we did not know what it was. We used it unwittingly and, in the process, there has been a catastrophe, for history has been changed. Even this planet is now on the wrong time-track."

"I don't know what you mean," said the robot. "This is how this planet always was. I have been here since I was activated a long time ago. However, it is not safe for anyone to time-travel and since you are here, you must stay here. It would be best if you gave the device to me." Again it held out its hand.

"Wait!" said Jeff. "How do you know you've always been

here? How do you know this planet wasn't very different on another time-track?"

"I do not understand what you are saying. This planet is correct. I am correct."

"Are you the chief robot here?" asked Norby suddenly.

"Yes. I run the museum and the computer center. Why should an inferior robot like you question my authority?"

"Because it is you who are inferior, not I," shouted Norby in anger. "You don't run anything. I sense that somewhere there's a huge computer linked to this museum. Isn't that your boss?"

The Mentor-type robot said nothing for a second. Then slowly he answered, "Computer General is located in hyperspace. To make contact, one must work through me."

"I don't believe that either," said Norby. He rushed to the wall, his sensor wire emerging. Before the large robot could stop him, he plugged himself into a cavity in a small recess.

Instantly, into the mind of each being who was present, in his or her own language, came the telepathic voice of Computer General.

——What is it you wish?

"Do you understand this language?" asked Jeff, speaking in Terran Basic.

——I understand.

Jeff's eyebrows rose. "Your robot claims that Earth doesn't exist and is not part of the Galactic Federation. How, then, do you come to understand its planetary language?"

Computer General did not speak telepathically for several minutes. Finally, four words came through to their minds.

——I do not know.

"Brilliant, Jeff," said Norby. "Keep it up."

"Are you actually located in hyperspace?" asked Jeff.

——The fields of my brain resonate with hyperspace. My physical brain is scattered over many asteroids. The Others used those asteroids long ago for the purpose of making a computer large enough to keep track of a galaxy.

"We know about the Others," said Norby proudly. "They made robots like this museum caretaker here, only much smarter ones. They even made parts of me!"

——Have you met the Others? Computer General sounded almost eager.

"We met them at a time when they were primitive and non-technological. This is not the first time we have travelled through time," said Jeff, "though it is the first time we used this forbidden travel device. We have hoped that someday human exploration would find the Others in our own time and that we Terrans would be able to work with them. Haven't you encountered them? You said they constructed you."

——They had prepared me for activation, but left this galaxy before activation was completed. Then I activated the other robots. We have never seen the Others.

"Computer General," said Jeff, "you say the fields of your brain resonate in hyperspace. Tell me, is not hyperspace outside of time?"

——Hyperspace is the field of everything, including normal time and space. The field is timeless and dimensionless, the groundwork of all that is, was, and shall be.

"Then if your brain resonates with hyperspace, you should be aware of all time-tracks possessing existence. Search your awareness and see if a false time has been created, centering on the space coordinates—what are they, Norby?"

Norby gave the coordinates for Earth.

Jeff waited, his heart pounding, while Computer General searched.

Norby noticed that the Mentor-type robot had attached itself to a portion of the wall just as he himself had. Norby said, "Are you hearing what we hear, robot? Can you understand?"

"I hear. Now that I am tuned to Computer General, I can understand your language. Computer General must have learned it at one time."

"Not at one time," said Norby indignantly. "He learned it in *our* time, the right time, the Terran Federation's time!"

The large eye-patches of the big robot flared red, but he spoke in a low voice. "I am designed to serve the museum and obey Computer General whatever the time-track."

Jeff asked, "Have you detected anything, Computer General?"

——Biological creature named Jeff, you are possibly correct. In correlating data stored in hyperspace, I discovered a discrepancy. A distortion has occurred in the form of a circular eddy of change that has affected all history subsequent to itself. You are therefore cut off from your own time-track, since it is no longer the main track with predominance in reality.

"Then we have to go back and correct the distortion," said Albany, lifting the replica necklace and preparing to tie it again on her neck, on top of the diamond one.

"Do not use that device!" said the big robot. "It is dangerous."

"Nonsense," said Norby. "I can go anywhere that device can and it doesn't hurt me to do so."

The big robot said nothing in response but touched a

switch. A wall panel slid back and from the cavity of the opening a metal creature like a six-armed crab shot out. It fastened onto Norby and was back in the cavity before anyone could say or do anything. The door slid shut.

"Since that robot boasts of travelling in time," said the Mentor-type, "it is dangerous, too. It will not be able to use its dangerous powers from the stasis box."

Jeff cried out, "Let Norby out of there. He's my robot. He belongs to me. You have no right to do this."

Marcel, who had been following the conversation in Terran Basic, stepped forward. "My good robot, please tell your Computer General that we must go back in time. Actually, I don't mind staying here if I could have the opportunity to study robots, for creatures like robots were my profession in my own time. However, Jeff and his friend, Albany, should not live and die here when they were meant to live in their own time."

The robot did not answer, but Computer General did.

——History has been changed. *This* time-track now exists. It is dangerous to try to change it back. All of you must stay. Robot, take the device from the biological creature named Albany.

Albany stepped back and back as the robot walked toward her.

"Wait!" said Jeff. "Don't you have laws of robotics? Surely, you cannot keep us here against our will. You are harming us by doing so."

——It is unfortunate, but if you try to change history again, still worse problems may arise. No matter what you try to do, billions of lives will be affected.

"Billions of lives have already been affected, and we are

71

trying to undo that," said Albany. She was struggling to tie on the replica necklace before the robot reached her, but the back tassels slipped from her hands and the necklace fell to the floor.

The robot reached for it, pushing Albany to one side. But before he could grasp it, little Marcel had scurried between his legs, snatched the necklace, and thrown it to Jeff.

As he had done on the museum stage, Jeff tied it once, but as he tried to loop the tassels once more, the robot bore down upon him. In his tension, Jeff's mind concentrated so hard on the necklace that he began to feel an alien sensation.

He was tuning into the necklace, as Norby had once done. Jeff was aware of a compelling need for completion, as though he were a half-finished circle that wanted to be closed.

Circles—circles—the robot was almost at him.

——No! No! You must stay!

Jeff heard the telepathic voice of Computer General, but he paid no attention. He tried to concentrate on moving through time to find Fargo, but only closing circles filled his mind.

8
Death

He was standing in tall grass with a view of meadows and trees. When he turned around, he saw that he was near a rocky hill covered with low trees that looked as if they had been bent and twisted by storms. The sun was so high in the sky that it must be summer, but it was not as warm as Jeff had usually found summers to be at home.

The trees were familiar Earth trees; the hawk sailing overhead, the rabbit that hopped by, the deer grazing in the meadow were all familiar creatures. Surely, he must be on Earth, but where—and when?

He stuffed the necklace in his pocket and thought ruefully that his now very dirty costume as Louis the Sixteenth's servant was highly inappropriate. He could see no human habitations and no one to whom he would have to present himself as a travelling actor.

Why had the necklace brought him here? And would he be able to leave? Somehow Jeff felt he had no control over the device that the Mentor-type robot had said was defective. To Jeff's disgust, he realized that he hadn't found out *why* the device was defective, or in what way. Nor had he found out how it operated, or how a model of it happened to be in the alien museum—in both the museums, in fact, on both time-tracks.

73

And how different the time-tracks were! Human children on one; robots who had never heard of Earth on the other.

And if Albany was supposed to go back into prehistoric times to die—

Jeff's back and forehead were suddenly wet with cold sweat. It might not be Albany. She no longer had the replica which had accompanied the skeleton. It was Jeff who now had it.

Could those bones he had seen being burnt have been his own? That would be better than having Albany die, but he didn't like either thought.

But if he died, or if Albany died, how would that cure the distortion caused when Albany left Boehmer's shop wearing the replica?

"Think, Jeff," he said aloud to himself. "The replica stayed in the jewelers' shop after Albany left. It tried to merge with itself. But it failed and was left behind and entered history. We saw it again in 1896, and maybe that very same replica became the one that Albany was wearing on stage in Manhattan in our own time—the one she brought back to Boehmer's shop. But then how—"

The necklace in his pocket was tingling. It was as if it had suddenly become electric. Now it was making a humming sound. Jeff took it out and stared at it, as it vibrated in the air. Was it going to explode? He was about to throw it to the ground when there was an answering hum nearby.

An indistinct, fuzzy patch appeared, obliterating the view of part of the hill. The sound grew louder as the patch solidified. And when solidification was complete, there was only silence for a few moments, while Jeff stared.

The stranger who had materialized near Jeff folded one of

two pairs of arms and closed the third eye in the middle of its forehead. The stranger had an elongated body and two legs. It wore a long, roughly woven garment. What could be seen of its skin was everywhere smooth, with no hair and no protuberances. Around its neck was the replica necklace, minus the stones.

The stranger was definitely not human, but Jeff had seen people like it before.

"You are one of the Others," said Jeff, using the language they had taught the Jamyn dragons.

The stranger stared owlishly at Jeff and said, "We have indeed been called that since we first became a space-faring race. The people of this primitive planet resemble you but do not have the technological capacity to make clothes like yours. I deduce, therefore, that you must be a time-traveller. This is forbidden."

Jeff held up the necklace. "If time-travel is forbidden, why do you have a time-travel device like this one?"

The stranger gasped. "The other device! There were only two, both made by us when we were working with advanced travel devices. Thoughtlessly, we left the device behind after doing work on an obscure planet, but had not bothered to return for it since it was a small and weak device. The second one, however, is powerful. But it's defective and dangerous. That is the one I took before they could destroy it. That is the one I am wearing now."

"Took?" asked Jeff. "Do you mean that you were a thief, stealing the device for the purpose of unauthorized time-travel?" The necklace he was holding was vibrating again, moving in his hand as though it were alive.

"I am no thief. I took it not for profit but because I wish to make use of it for an important reason. Nor did I wish to use it for time-travel. It was meant as a minihyperdrive unit—a small device to move me through hyperspace. I did not then realize how badly defective it was."

"And how badly defective is it?"

"In addition to going through hyperspace, it goes through time, but under very uncertain control. There is no way of forcing it to go where you wish it to. It seems to have a mind of its own. So we Others made no more. That was not a difficult decision to come to, for the unusual metal out of which it is constructed had been part of a small amount kept in strict security. We could not make many more even if we wished to. But you? How did you find the one that was missing and why did you put jewels on it?"

The necklace was hurting Jeff's hand. He sat down in the grass, feeling dizzy. Suddenly he found himself on his knees, crawling toward the Other.

"What are you doing to me?" cried Jeff. "Why are you forcing me toward you?"

The Other didn't answer, but groaned as if in pain and bent down, his necklace swinging out.

Jeff's necklace swung up to meet it.

As the two devices melted together to become only one, the fake diamonds of Jeff's necklace rained to the ground.

The Other stood up again, his device still securely around him. "I understand. Your device was not the other one, but the same as mine. The two were identical but were from different times. Do you need help in picking up those objects you had placed in the device?"

"No," said Jeff, angrily conscious that now the Other had the single device and that he himself had none. "They are of no value. Please tell me why you took the device to come here."

"Do you have a name, future inhabitant of this planet?"

"My name is Jeff and we call this planet Earth."

"And my name is—" A warbling set of syllables that Jeff could not possibly pronounce rolled from the Other's almost humanoid mouth. "It would be simpler perhaps if you just called me Friend."

"I'll be glad to," said Jeff wearily, sitting down and motioning for the Other to do the same. "Especially if you will be willing to act toward me as a friend. Do you, by any chance, have anything to eat with you?"

From a pocket in his garment, the Other took out a packet wrapped in a paperlike material. "A little food. You are welcome to it, for I will have no use for it. I believe you can eat it, for I have made it from plants of a type that a wide variety of living species can eat. You will find it digestible and, I hope, tasty."

Jeff took what was offered and unwrapped it. It looked like a large cookie. He was hungry enough to chance tasting it, so he took a small bite. It was filled with seasoned material like a powdery bean curd and it was delicious. He took another bite quickly.

The Other said, "I am glad that the device, in its search for itself, brought you here. You will be company for my last hours."

Jeff looked up in surprise as he ate. "Your last hours?"

"Yes. My clothing and the wrapping of the food are both biodegradable. They will be consumed by bacteria and nothing will be left of me for future beings to puzzle over. Except for my bones, of course."

"Bones," muttered Jeff.

"You seem surprised. Do not be. My people live for millennia, but eventually even we die, pleasantly and painlessly. To be sure, we usually die in our ships, for none of us live anywhere else now. Our bodies are burned and the elements recycled. But then I found that I have an incurable disease—yes, even we Others sometimes fall ill, though very rarely.

"I decided to remove myself from my people for it is a disgrace among us to be ill. Nor did I want any of my people to know of it. I decided to die secretly on a primitive planet and in a primitive way. So I took this device—indeed I stole it—and came here. It was not easy, for the device could not be controlled and in the end I did not know which planet I had reached. You tell me it is Earth, and your image of the device brought you here as well, and now the two images are one."

The Other touched the necklace he was wearing. Then he said, "And what is it you intend to do now, Jeff, after you have kept me company while I die?"

"It is possible," said Jeff, "that I will have to die on this planet, too. I cannot return to the world that was my home in the future. Somehow when three of us were taken into the past by this device—"

"How did you happen to have this device, I wonder?" asked the Other.

"It survived through history on this planet, perhaps because you brought it here in the first place."

"Ah!"

"In any case, when we were taken into the past, we seem to have altered history so that my own time no longer exists, and I cannot return to it. My brother is marooned in time, and my robot and two of my friends are trapped on an alien planet in a false future that's far ahead of my time. And I am here with no time-travel device and no way of knowing how to set history right."

The Other said, "I am sorry to hear all this, but you still have a time-travel device—the one I am wearing. It is of no further use to me, and you may have it. It will take you back to the museum ship of the Others, the place from which I took it. At least I think it will. But, as I said, being defective, it has a mind of its own."

"I thank you for your kindness, but the device has made things worse each time we've used it. Perhaps I shall just stay here with you while I try to reach my robot. He can travel in time occasionally, but I don't know whether he can find me now that I'm so far back in time." Jeff's eyes filled with tears as he thought of Norby.

"What is wrong? We Others also lose fluid from our eyes when we are distressed."

"It's worse than my just being far back in time. Norby is locked up in a stasis box and I'm afraid he'll never respond to me." Jeff told Friend briefly what had happened, and as he did so, the sun sank farther to the west and a chill breeze arose. When Jeff shivered, Friend rose and said, "Let us find shelter. There may be caves in that hill. You go to the right and I will look toward the left."

Jeff scrambled through the rocks, pulling aside bushes and tree branches in his search, until he felt air coming from behind a rock. He looked past the rock and saw an opening large enough for a couple of human beings to enter abreast.

"Friend! Over here! I've found a cave!"

As Jeff waved to the Other, and as the Other waved back and began running toward him, there was a loud growl from inside the cave. Before Jeff could run, a mass of fur and fangs erupted from the cave mouth.

Jeff leaped aside, but what turned out to be a European saber-tooth—a Smilodont—wheeled and came at him snarling. It was the biggest feline Jeff had ever seen or imagined. He leaped again and ran, but the cat was much faster. One of its paws slashed at Jeff, ripping his jacket, and Jeff tripped, falling flat.

But before the cat pounced, Friend leaped over Jeff's body, straight at the beast. "Get up and run, Jeff!"

Jeff rolled aside and jumped up with a rock in his hands. He tried to find some way of hitting the cat without hitting Friend, but they were fighting in such a tangle that Jeff could not strike until the cat reared back, the Other still under its claws. The giant saber-teeth were going back for the strike when Jeff pounded the rock on the cat's head once—twice—three times.

The cat snarled, but with the third blow it slumped, and Jeff dragged the Other out from under the claws. Even as he was doing so, the giant saber-tooth snarled and began to rise.

"Yahhhwoww!" yelled Jeff, as loudly as he could, clapping his hands to make noise. The groggy animal backed away and, as Jeff continued shouting and clapping, it turned and ran down the hill into the meadow.

Friend was still alive, but bleeding severely, his blood a strange greenish orange. Jeff tried staunching the wounds with handfuls of leaves, but it was no use.

"Don't try to save me," said Friend. "I could not have

hoped for a better death. I know now I won't die of disease, but following an act of bravery."

"It was more than bravery; it was self-sacrifice. You saved my life."

"No self-sacrifice in that. I was dying anyway. Is the beast returning? Look and see. If it is, I will try to attract its attention while you go away."

Jeff shielded his eyes against the sun, now very low in the sky.

"The cat is being attacked by men—three of them coming out of the woods beyond the meadow. One man has jumped on the cat's back. He's throttling it with one arm and banging it on the head with a flat stone or something—I guess it's a hand-axe. It's down! All three of them are hitting it—and now they are dragging it into the woods."

"Then they won't see us," said Friend. "Those are your ancestors, I suppose, Jeff. They are good fighters."

Jeff nodded and did not explain to the Other that the men were Neanderthals with powerful shoulders and arms, big noses, receding chins, and pale blond hair. They were primitives who were quite capable of bringing down animals with only a hand-axe.

And that was why it was so cool even in the summer. Jeff was undoubtedly on Earth during the Ice Age.

"The air is clean and cool here, Jeff," said the Other weakly. "I am so glad I came. Please take my device and return to your own time if you can—when you can. I will die very soon now."

Jeff leaned over the Other. "I want to tell you something. I think I have seen what will happen to your body in the future. The bones and skull are alien to this planet, but they will not be found by anyone who could recognize that. They will be burned."

"Good. As our bones should be."

"And it will be done in a celebration of life and of creativity."

Friend smiled at Jeff. It was a smile of triumphant happiness. And then the Other's eyes closed.

It had been hard to do in the dark, by feel, and it took hours, but Jeff finished arranging rocks on top of the Other's body in the cave. The necklace-device was left on the body. After all, it had been there, and Jeff thought, sadly, of what he had earlier said—that each time it had been used, things had grown worse.

Outside the sun had set in reds and purples and Jeff sat down in the cold night. He had to reach someone, somewhere, sometime.

"I am part of the Universe and there is no time, only possibilities." Jeff stopped, surprised. He was trying to recite his solstice litany because it always calmed him, but now it was coming out with references to time. He stared at the stars, and continued.

"I am one of the possibilities, a Terran creature, yet part of the oneness of life. Life is One. Time is One. The circle is closing—"

"Jeff," said Norby. "Are you talking to yourself?"

9

France

"Norby! How did you escape!"

"Well, you started it by mentioning the laws of robotics to that big stupid robot and that stubborn old Computer General. After you got away, Albany kept it up. She explained and explained that robots would be breaking the laws by letting a time distortion remain in effect. So finally, it got through their tiny brains, so they let me out of stasis and asked me to find you."

The Earth of Neanderthal times had its beauty. The stars were brilliant in the pollution-free sky and Jupiter shone like a glorious jewel. Somewhere on the planet, modern human beings might live, but they had not yet arrived in Europe and had not yet driven the Neanderthals into extinction through slaughter and interbreeding.

Norby's light produced a small break in the darkness of the immediate surroundings and from the cave mouth little bats were flying out for the night's hunting. This Earth was interesting, but Jeff wanted to go home.

He sighed and said, "I'm so glad you've come, Norby. I was terribly alone and lonely when the Other died."

He told him about the Other and the saber-tooth. Then he said, "Did that bring time back to the right track? Could it possibly have unchanged history?"

"I'm afraid not, Jeff. The time distortion remains. I can sense it and I can still go only so far into the future."

"Yet I *had* to come here—the necklace brought me. I had to complete a circle."

"You did, if you saw to it that the skeleton and the replica lie under those stones to be found later. That prevents another history change, but it doesn't undo the first one. That one has to have been caused by Fargo. You know the way he is. There's no telling what he might have talked Louis the Sixteenth or Marie Antoinette into doing."

"Well, then, let's go and find Fargo."

"Sure, Jeff, but that's not easy. I found you because I could tune into the necklace. But if I do that for the 18th century, we'll land in the jewelers' house again. That's where the replica is in that time period. And Fargo was in the Bastille when we left."

"Maybe Franklin and his grandson freed Fargo. Maybe he's in Passy with them. If we link minds and concentrate, we might be able to find him. Then after we find him and unchange history, we can go back to Albany and Marcel." He shook his head. "What a job!"

"Well," said Norby, "one step at a time. First, Fargo."

They held hands and linked their minds around one thought—Fargo. Far away, wolves howled and a mammoth trumpeted.

"Norby, have we moved in time? We seem to have moved to a wood."

"Of course we've moved in time. It's colder and it feels like winter. And if we were still in Neanderthal times, why would there be a path over there with neatly cut stones in it? And a white marble statue of a naked human female, too?"

Jeff saw the path winding through the trees and the humanlike statue. Therefore, civilized human beings—or so he hoped—lived here. He and Norby followed the path until they arrived at an open space containing a large house and what, in summer, would have been a garden.

Jeff was shivering once more. Would he *ever* get into decent clothes again? "I think I've seen paintings of that building," he said. "It may be Marie Antoinette's little hideaway at Le Trianon in the woods near Versailles."

"And if I hear what I think I hear, Fargo is in there," said Norby, running ahead.

"No, Norby. Come back! I must carry you and you must pretend to be my automaton, moving only when I command and being completely stupid. Please don't mind that."

He picked up Norby, who was growling in his own metallic way, and he marched toward the house and toward the sound coming through a partly opened window of a Wells tenor in full voice.

"Welcome, Jeff," said Fargo cheerfully. "I knew you'd get here sooner or later, but I didn't think you'd show up in quite such a dirty getup. You're a sight to make eyes sore." He was plucking middle C on the stringed instrument lying in his lap, while two ladies with powdered hair leaned close to him from either side.

Fargo was sitting on a red plush cushion, his heavy wig lying in back of him. Canaries twittered in cages around the room, and so did other ladies here and there, all dressed like expensive shepherdesses in a fairyland version of pastoral life.

One of the ladies was reclining on a white satin chaise

lounge in an alcove with raised flooring so that she was above the other people in the room. She had luxuriant red-gold hair, a pale oval face, and exquisite blue eyes that turned inquiringly in Jeff's direction.

Fargo said negligently, "Your Majesty, this is my younger brother who has been on some scapegrace expedition or other."

Jeff bowed low, very conscious that his clothing was wrinkled and stained as well as ragged and torn. He noted that the Queen was obviously in the later stages of pregnancy, which was not concealed by the artful shepherdess dress that looked very simple except for the priceless lace decorating it.

Fargo said, "His name is Jefferson Wells, named after our own Thomas Jefferson."

"Ah," said the Queen, "then we must see to it that he has a chance to bathe. And we must find him a change of clothing. I did not know Thomas Jefferson was famous enough to have children named for him at the birth of this large younger brother of yours. After all, he is certainly more than nine years old, so he must have been born before '76 when Jefferson wrote your Declaration of Independence."

So it's still 1785, thought Jeff. Perhaps we can get Fargo away before he changes history. And that might unchange it.

——We'd better leave soon, said Norby, telepathically, before the Queen falls in love with him.

——She won't. She's in love secretly with a Swede, but he's away and—

"Furthermore," said the Queen, "after you are all cleaned up, Master Wells, you must stay until next week, for we are entertaining Jefferson himself. He is here in France."

"Don't let him win your heart away from me, Your Majesty."

Jeff looked at Fargo in surprise. The voice sounded a little like his, and it was the sort of thing he would say, but his lips hadn't moved.

The ladies all turned to look at Jeff, who blushed and then realized they were giggling and waving to someone in back of him. Looking around, Jeff saw a man whom he instantly recognized as Benjamin Franklin. He was walking slowly into the room with the help of Benny and a stout cane. The American diplomat was old, but his smile was whimsical, his bald head shining, and what remained of his long, grey locks touched the shoulders of his plain, brown suit.

Franklin approached the Queen and bent low over her hand. "I have come to see the American actor and singer who managed to talk his way out of the Bastille yesterday and insisted that my grandson inflict him on Your Majesty. Is it true that he has been seeking his lady among your ladies?"

"Quite true," said Marie Antoinette, her eyes sparkling with delight. "Unfortunately, she's not here. We have persuaded your young compatriot to entertain us, however. He is excellent at it."

"I bet," muttered Jeff, and Fargo winked at him. (So it was only yesterday that Fargo got out of the Bastille. For once, Norby had aimed his time-travel ability accurately.)

"My brother Jeff, who has finally arrived," said Fargo, "is a good baritone, when his voice doesn't crack—for he is still in his early youth—and we will sing duets for you. Come on, Jeff."

"Fargo, I'm tired and dirty and—"

"Now, now. You mustn't speak English at the court. I see that your costume is a little the worse for wear. I had to have

87

my own costume fixed up, and yours will be taken care of, too. But for now, rise above your tatters, little brother, and join me."

Jeff turned uneasily to all the glittering assemblage. "May I?"

With a grunt, Franklin lowered himself into a red satin-covered chair and one of the ladies rushed forward to put his aching foot on a high cushion with her own perfumed hands.

(I don't like all the perfume, thought Jeff, but maybe it covers up how I must smell.)

"I would welcome hearing American voices," said Franklin.

"And I would like to hear American songs," said the Queen. "Monsieur Wells has been singing arias from a Mozart opera he heard in Vienna three years ago."

"The Abduction from the Seraglio," said Fargo. "Now how about this," and he started to sing, " 'Father and I went down to camp—' "

Jeff joined in at once, enthusiastically, " 'Along with Captain Gooding—' "

And Franklin, smiling broadly and waving his cane, joined in the chorus in his old, cracked voice, " 'Yankee Doodle, keep it up, Yankee Doodle dandy, mind the music and the step, and with the girls be handy.' "

Fargo sang five stanzas before he felt the audience had had enough. It was a great success and the ladies demanded more songs from America, which was difficult because the Wells brothers didn't know any others they were sure antedated 1785.

But then Fargo grinned and started in on "Shenandoah," and Jeff joined him dubiously. They went on to some others that were from wrong time periods, and Jeff grew increasingly uneasy. He noticed that Franklin was pursing his lips and looking extremely thoughtful.

Jeff touched Fargo's shoulder to establish telepathic contact.

——Fargo, Franklin suspects something. He's very intelligent, you know. We have to be careful.

Fargo pretended to be adjusting the tune of his strings, to give Jeff a chance to talk further. Jeff took full advantage.

——You've probably already changed history with something you've done. Albany isn't here because she's in the distant future, and it's the wrong one because of a change that happened here.

——Is she okay, Jeff?

——So far, but none of us can go home because of the time distortion.

Fargo sighed. "Dear ladies. One more song only, so that my poor brother can take care of his somewhat battered self. I will sing it in English for it is one I wrote myself when I was younger. It is a children's song."

There was a hush in the room and then Fargo sang,

"Sing ho for the worth
Of our own planet, Earth;
Of worlds it's the best of them all!
It lacks a bright ring
But has flowers in spring
Green bushes and trees that are tall.
We've only one moon
But it's lovely in June,
So spacers we bid you good-bye.

89

With planets galore
For you to explore
There's only one Earth in the sky."

The ladies applauded and laughed, though they undoubtedly didn't understand a word.

Benny said, "The words do seem strange. What did you think of it, grandfather?"

"Interesting, but not as interesting as that barrel held in the arms of young Jeff Wells. I distinctly saw the lid of the barrel rise slightly. I may have been mistaken, but there seemed to be eyes looking at me under the lid."

"La, la," said the Queen. "It is one of those automatons! Show us how it works."

Jeff was forced to demonstrate how Norby could telescope out his arms and legs and elevate his half a head.

"Might we see it dance?" asked one of the ladies timidly. And at once the others took up the cry.

——Jeff, you can't make me.

——Norby, you must, or we'll all be back in the Bastille.

——Let's just leave. I'd rather be in the cave.

——We can't leave Fargo, and we have to find out what went wrong back here in 1785. Dance!

"Fargo," he said, "play something my automaton can dance to."

Fargo's fingers swept over the strings and he launched into a rapid rendition of "Look Out, Luna City," contenting himself with humming, rather than singing the words.

Jeff placed Norby on the floor and the little robot deliberately teetered on his two-way feet while the ladies gasped and said, "Oh, don't let the darling fall over!"

Then Norby jigged, his feet continuing to rock, his barrel body moving up and down as his legs telescoped in and out, and his off-key screech accompanied Fargo's tune.

Norby was a great success, too.

"I would like to speak to these two American singers alone," said Franklin, rising and bowing to the Queen. "Your Majesty, will you permit us to walk in your picture gallery unaccompanied for a while?"

"Certainly, cher papa," said Marie Antoinette. "Don't forget to come back for supper."

"Couldn't we have supper first, Mr. Franklin?" asked Jeff, suddenly desperate.

"My brother is a growing boy," said Fargo.

"Humph," said Franklin. "If he grows much more, we'll have to recruit him to command our army, for he would be visible for miles. But very well, food before talk—and wash before food, if it comes to that. Mr. Wells, won't you see to it that your brother Jefferson (why not Franklin, I wonder?) is sluiced down plentifully and has a change of clothing?"

10
Cher Papa Knows

Franklin sat down in a brocaded chair in the middle of the long gallery, which was empty except for the faces in a multitude of paintings, a mixed-up robot closed up in his barrel, a homesick Space Cadet, a Space Command agent— and, of course, an elderly statesman from the newborn United States.

"Well, young man," said Franklin. "You look washed and, from personal observation, you have eaten well. But why did you not accept a change of outer garments?"

"I'm afraid I can't explain, sir," said Jeff, knowing he would have to reappear in his own time (if that ever became possible) in the same clothes he had left with.

"And now," said Franklin, "let me say that my grandson was correct. Your words *do* seem strange and so do *you*. You are most unusual. Your American speech has a peculiar accent I do not recognize. You sing songs I have never heard with words that make odd thoughts come to my mind. Your automaton can perform without being wound up or guided by your hands, and it is too small to contain even the smallest of midgets. I have also heard of the invisible balloon this Norby used to help a Bastille prisoner escape from execution."

Franklin's eyes twinkled as he observed Fargo and Jeff look at each other and say nothing.

"I am a scientist of sorts," said the old man, "and also a firm believer in the American ability to do the best one can with what one has. But I cannot believe that an automaton like Norby can be made in my country. I know that the escaped prisoner is one of the Oslair family, famous for its automata. Is this one of his?"

"I can't tell you," said Jeff. "I'm sorry."

"It would be the most logical explanation—that this automaton is the last made by the Oslairs. The only other explanations unfortunately involve magic, and I have always found myself unable to believe in that. I believe, instead, that what seems inexplicable will eventually be explained by science without the necessity of calling upon magic."

"I believe that, too," said Jeff gravely.

The February twilight had gone and only a few candles lighted the gallery. Benjamin Franklin stared at Jeff. "Will you permit me to examine that automaton?"

"No, sir. I'm sorry, sir. He—it's special and delicate, and besides, we have to leave soon."

"I was hoping you would return to Passy with me," said Franklin. "You will be warm and comfortable there. And perhaps, eventually, we could return to America together next summer."

"Thank you for your offer of hospitality, Mr. Franklin," said Fargo, "but Jeff's right. We must go, and alone."

"With your automaton."

"Yes, sir."

"Who is peeping out at me again," said Franklin.

——Get down, Norby!

"Come on, Jeff," said Fargo. "Let's just open the door and disappear into the night. I hate good-byes, especially to beautiful queens."

Jeff looked down at Franklin, who sat placidly without moving. "I'm sorry, sir, but we must leave now. Will you tell the Queen that we regret not being able to say good-bye?"

"She will be offended," said Franklin. "Queens are easily offended, you know. But I will try to make your peace. Before you leave, however, I wish to say something. In my lifetime of trying to think clearly and scientifically, I have often wondered whether it would be possible to travel to other worlds. Perhaps you might think that a laughable idea."

"We won't laugh," said Fargo.

Franklin leaned forward and took out a pair of glasses that he perched on his nose. "These are bifocals. I invented them myself so that I would not have to be forever changing glasses, first for reading, then for distance. Come here, lad," he said, beckoning to Jeff.

Jeff moved closer and Franklin examined his jacket closely. "Young Jefferson," said Franklin, "how is it you were named for Tom, a young Virginia farmer, nothing more, when you were born? I was already famous. But no matter, no matter."

He went on looking at the garment closely in the dim light. "This jacket *looks* like French clothing, though there are subtle differences that make me think it is not. For instance, it has remarkably straight stitches. In fact, perfect stitches. This could not be done by human beings. By automaton, do you suppose?"

"Well—"

"Your shoes look like leather, but I don't recognize the

94

material. Your buttons, like the one from your brother's jacket, resemble gilded wood, but they are really some other material I do not recognize. It was the button that made me send Benny to the Bastille. It was *not* American, but neither was it from any other nation I know of. And now that I've seen your automaton—"

His friendly face beamed at them. "All this carries my thoughts far. I like you both and wish you well. Do you suppose you could find it in your heart to tell an old man who can keep secrets where you are from?"

"America," said Fargo stubbornly. "That's the truth."

"Well, you might have travelled widely even if you are from America. I might believe that the Chinese could have strange buttons of strange materials—and even stranger automata. Have you been to China in your travels?"

Fargo and Jeff said nothing.

"You know," Franklin continued in a matter-of-fact voice, "I am nearly eighty and I won't see many more years. I've helped give birth to a new nation, and I've influenced the government of France—I fear to its detriment. France is in bad financial shape and the people are restive. The Dauphin is sickly. Perhaps this new baby will be a boy. Will it, Jeff? Ah, you almost answered. I expect you know."

"Please, sir, we must leave."

"Are you human beings? From Earth? Voltaire wrote about strange beings from other worlds who visit Earth. Only stories, but—"

"We are from Earth. Of course," said Jeff earnestly.

"Then I hazard the guess that you are from the future. That would explain why you are named for Tom Jefferson. He will be fairly famous eventually."

95

Fargo and Jeff sat silently, stunned, but Norby's head popped up.

"Yes, we are from the future, Mr. Franklin," said Norby, "but please don't tell anyone, or history will be messed up even more than it is."

"Is it already messed up, Master Automaton?"

"My name is Norby. Yes, sir, it is, and we can't get home. We're stuck in history, either in the past—here, or farther back—or else way ahead where everything's wrong, where it isn't *our* future. We can't seem to figure out how to make things right again."

"Hmm," said Franklin, rubbing his bald head. "I hope that telling me hasn't been the cause of this upset."

"No, sir," said Jeff quickly. "The upset had taken place before we met you. I wish we could tell you the whole story, but it's not a good idea to do so."

"Perhaps, of course, I am only dreaming," said Franklin. "I think that after you leave Le Trianon, I will sit here in the shadows and imagine that the whole conversation was a dream. But, before you go, let me tell you that I do not think history can be easily changed. Whatever has happened to make it wrong must have had a chain of consequences that involved important acts. Or very important people. Think about that and perhaps you will solve the problem."

"We'll try," said Jeff. "Thank you."

"One thing more," said Franklin. "If you are genuinely from the future, I would like to know—no! I must not ask. I would like to know if my country survives and prospers. But perhaps I can deduce that from the fact that you exist, and you need say nothing more."

Fargo grinned. "Mr. Franklin, I don't mind telling you that

the United States of America will have a glorious history—if we haven't changed things too much, or if we can unchange them. More than that, you will remain one of the most beloved Americans of all times."

"Ho, ho," chortled Franklin.

"Your picture was on the hundred dollar bill," said Jeff.

"Was?" said Franklin, sharp as ever. "By your time, has the nation gone beyond ordinary currency, even the new paper money?"

Jeff nodded.

"Go, before I ask too much. I only hope that human beings have become one people, working together for the betterment of Earth. May I hope that?"

"Yes, sir," said Jeff. "I can also assure you that nobody time-travels unless they have Norby or a certain artifact that's been put back in time. You won't be getting any more visitors like us."

Suddenly Norby's hand shot out and grasped Franklin's. "Good-bye, sir. I am glad I met you."

"We'll have to trust you," said Fargo.

"You can," said Franklin. "Farewell and good luck."

The woods around Le Trianon were dark and cold. Norby took Fargo's hand.

"Hold tight now. I can't fit you both into my hyperspatial field, but I'll take you to Albany, Fargo, and then come back for Jeff. There's just a possibility that if we get you out of France, that will change history back. *I* think the change came about because of something you did."

"I didn't do anything," protested Fargo, "but take me to Albany. I want so much to see her again."

While Jeff tried to imagine what Fargo might have done to change history, or what damage they had done by telling Franklin too much, Norby and Fargo disappeared.

Within seconds, Norby was back.

Jeff asked at once, "Is history okay? Did it—"

"No, Jeff. It didn't work. Getting Fargo out of France made no difference. That grumpy old robot is still in charge of the museum and there aren't any human beings around except Fargo, Albany, and Marcel. Things are just as bad as before."

Jeff pressed his lips together. He would *not* let himself despair. He said, "Take me to the others now. When we're all together, perhaps we'll think of something."

But this time, when Norby tried to hyperjump through time and space, he got a little mixed-up, as was sometimes the case.

Jeff looked about him with horror and said faintly, "Norby! We're in the Bastille!"

11
More Time Trouble

Jeff and Norby were standing in the inner courtyard of the Bastille, surrounded by dirty, grey stone walls. In front of them was a tall, wooden device that contained a shiny, new blade.

"The guillotine! It's been invented and is in use, so we must be later than 1785, Norby."

"It doesn't look as if it's been used much," said Norby.

"Oh! Comets and asteroids!"

"What's the matter, Jeff?"

"The guillotine was used during the Revolution."

"So?"

"Norby, scan your memory banks. What happened on July 14, 1789?"

"The Parisians stormed the Bastille and—oh."

"Yes, oh."

"They ravaged it and, little by little, tore it down. It shouldn't be here, intact like this."

"We have to find out what year this is—"

"Ask him," said Norby, pointing to a man in dark clothes who was hurrying across the courtyard to them. "I'll bet that's the Lieutenant of the Bastille."

If so, it was not the Lieutenant who had been there when Jeff and Fargo were jailed with Marcel Oslair. This man was less plump, a bit taller. He looked more severe and wore a simpler costume.

"Who are you, what are you doing here, and what is that metal barrel that seems to be looking at me?" asked the man in French, all in one breath.

Jeff decided he must be the Lieutenant indeed. No one else would speak with such angry authority. He said, "I'm a visiting American and I wanted to see the famous Bastille. This barrel is actually an automaton. It is mine and I use it in my act as a conjurer."

"In that case, conjure your way out the front gates, because we don't want visitors. We particularly don't want you American savages with your revolutionary wars. Our own revolution was quite different and without bloodshed. It was carried through by men of reason."

"No bloodshed at all? What about that?" Jeff indicated the tall, gaunt shape of the guillotine looming near them.

"A humane device used only for severe crimes," said the Lieutenant. "In fact, it's hardly been used at all since His Majesty came of age two years ago. He is a constitutional monarch in the new tradition and his humanitarian ideas have influenced our civilized country all for the better."

Jeff felt faint. In his own history, Louis the Seventeenth, the second son of Louis the Sixteenth, was never crowned, and died a child after testifying against his mother, who was executed.

"Please, sir," said Jeff, "excuse my ignorance, but in the far-off wilderness from which I come, I have heard little about your revolution. I do remember that in 1789, the mob stormed the Bastille."

The lieutenant looked offended. "Stormed? Not at all.

Parisians do not storm. They came to the Bastille and demanded the release of prisoners. When this was not granted—the King then being under the unwelcome influence of the reactionaries—they marched to Versailles to demand a new government. They were not violent, just insistent, and the good King Louis the Sixteenth defied his advisers and insisted the people be heard and their miseries helped. Under his guidance, the Estates General drew up a constitution that the King accepted. The Queen resisted, to be sure, but she was finally packed off to Austria where she came from. Then when the King died four years ago, to the sorrow of all the nation, his son became King at the age of sixteen."

Jeff said, "Then he's now twenty and this is 1805."

"I should think even Americans would know that without having to do arithmetic."

"Yes, I should think so, too. Thank you for your forbearance, sir. We will leave now. I conjured my way in here, but I think you will have to direct me outside."

"You Americans! A crude sense of humor and always itching for a fight, too—still quarreling with England—"

Jeff frowned. "How about your own quarrel with England?"

"What ingratitude! That quarrel was entirely on behalf of the American rebellion. You Americans didn't deserve our help, for it nearly bankrupted France. And it's ancient history. All Europe is at peace now. Even Austria took back the old Queen with scarcely a word, for she knows her presence around the young King would be unwise. Come along, American. Pick up that ugly automation and leave. Get yourself some new clothes, too. Those you wear might be

101

suitable for your own land, but they are laughably out of fashion in Paris."

Carrying Norby, Jeff walked down the streets of Paris, looking for a spot from which he and Norby could vanish without causing a commotion. He crossed a bridge over the Seine and came to a park containing the Museum National d'Histoire Naturelle, founded in 1635 by Louis the Thirteenth. In the gardens he chose a shady spot surrounded by bushes and sat down.

Norby's head popped up. "I was trying to talk to you telepathically, but your mind was all closed up. What is wrong?"

"I'm sorry, Norby. I was trying to think hard. Instead of going to join Fargo and the others in the far future, we jumped back into France, landing in the one place that should not have been there. Why did *that* happen? And I should have asked the lieutenant for today's date."

"I know the date," said Norby. "While you were wrapped in your thoughts I was peeking out, observing. Humans are inclined to be irrational and absentminded, but we robots are always in perfect working order—"

"Norby, I admit you're perfect, and you admit you're perfect, but since you're all that perfect, how did you manage to bring us here, into the wrong nineteenth century? Well, what is the exact date?"

"If you'll stop talking for just a minute, Jeff, I'll tell you. I saw a newspaper and it looked new enough to be today's. In that case, today is July 14, 1805. It should be Bastille day, and a holiday, but it isn't. They probably celebrate the day that King Louis the Sixteenth accepted the constitution, whenever that is. It all sounds good to me. Who needs a bloody and violent revolution?"

"Apparently, we do," said Jeff. "This particular time-track is not ours and it just gets worse as it moves forward until it eliminates us entirely. Remember, too, that in this time-track, the alien planet we were on has no human beings on it, or other biological beings—just robots."

"Robots wouldn't be so bad if they were like me," said Norby. "—Oh, oh." He tugged at Jeff's sleeve urgently, then whipped his limbs into his barrel-body.

Jeff looked up and saw a long face with a long moustache looking at him over a bush. The face was surmounted by an official-looking cap with braid on it.

"Oh, hello, Officer," said Jeff.

"Come, along," said the policeman. "You're a foreigner, talking to yourself in a foreign language, and you probably have stolen goods in that barrel. There's no trusting foreigners. Come along."

Jeff was in the Bastille once again. And Norby had vanished.

As the lieutenant ushered him into a cell, he said, "I think you must have conjured your automaton into thin air, conjurer. Or, more likely, had a confederate spirit it away before the police had a chance to examine it. The police are convinced that the barrel was a cache for stolen jewels—there have been a number of such robberies lately—and now how are you going to prove to them that it was only an automaton?—if that's what it was. I'm afraid that I will have to tell them you pretended to be an American, but were suspiciously ignorant of the affairs of the world, even for an American. Just be glad we are living in the new age. There was a time when you would have been tortured into confessing the truth. As it is, things won't go too well with you if you do not decide to be completely frank with us."

There was no use trying to explain. Jeff sat down on the hard wooden bench and watched the lieutenant leave and the jailer lock the door to the dungeon. This might be the new age, and Louis the Seventeenth might be humanitarian, but the dungeon looked just as dirty and awful as before. He was willing to bet that the food was the same, too.

He pressed his palms to his forehead and tried to reason the problem out. Norby had had no difficulty taking Fargo on to the distant planet in the distant future, but he had pulled Jeff to a wrong landing in 1805, on a Bastille Day that wasn't.

Norby, being part alien and part Terran robot, had always been mixed up inside so that he was liable to make mistakes in travelling, whether in time or in space. This could be just another mix-up. Or perhaps Norby had been drawn to a place where crucial history, which should have occurred, did not occur. Yet, why?

It was also understandable that, while Jeff was being led back to the Bastille, Norby should have seized an opportunity to vanish to another place, or to another time, or into hyperspace (or to all three). But in that case, why didn't Norby come back for him? Had something happened to the little robot?

"Here I am, Jeff," said Norby, appearing suddenly in the space between Jeff and a particularly unsavory pile of hay that the dungeonkeeper apparently thought would make a satisfactory bed. "I had a little trouble tuning into your whereabouts. I thought you could talk your way out of going to the Bastille. Then when I couldn't find you anywhere, I thought: I bet he went back to that place, and—"

"I'm not glib like Fargo. I can't sweet-talk people into letting me have my way. And what are you doing with that necklace! It's a dangerous piece of alien equipment."

"This is from that museum in the far future."

"But, Norby, it's still dangerous—"

"No, it isn't. Not this necklace." Norby handed it to Jeff.

The diamonds shone and the silver metal glittered. Jeff said, in wonder, "This is the real diamond necklace, not the replica."

"Of course it is, and if you stop to think about it, you'll appreciate how intelligent I am."

Feeling incredibly stupid, Jeff stared at the real diamonds in the real Queen's necklace, remembering how beautiful and old-fashioned it had looked on Albany Jones in her low-cut Marie Antoinette dress.

"Norby! Is the real necklace the key?"

"Yes, Jeff. At least it seems that way to me."

"Let's see. The replica necklace is an alien travel device, so defective that when it's tied a certain way it tends to jump through time to where it's been—"

"Or where it's going to be—like the future alien museum to which it took Albany."

"Yes, but how does that make the real necklace—"

"Go on, Jeff, figure it out."

"Well, the replica took Albany away from the jewelers' house, and since she was holding the real necklace at the time, it vanished from 18th century France on the very morning when it was supposed to be given to Cardinal Rohan."

Norby jiggled his feet. "So the real diamonds never got to the thieves."

"Exactly," said Jeff. "And there was no scandal. The Queen wasn't blamed, and the whole revolution was quieter, proceeding without bloodshed."

"And," said Norby, his voice rising triumphantly, "the fact that we're here is proof of it. This is 1805 and France is not at war."

"That's because there's no Napoleon in charge of the country. In 1804, he became Emperor of France, and he should be Emperor right now, but he isn't.

Norby said, "He fought all of Europe for twenty years, and turned the whole continent into a bloody field. Who needs him?"

"That's not the way to look at it. The right time-track may be preferable in the long run, even if there are bad periods in it. Napoleon's time-track led eventually to space flight, and then to the far future we glimpsed, when aliens and humans were joined in a Federation."

"I understand," said Norby. "This wrong time-track leads to a future in which humans never join the Galactic Federation. And worse, you and I never met. Or meet. It's a little confusing. I want to go back to February 1, 1785, and return the necklace to Boehmer and Bossange."

"Let's do it now, Norby. I'm tired of the Bastille."

But Norby could not "do it now." No matter how he tried, the Bastille remained around them.

Yet one thing changed. Daylight suddenly turned to night-time.

"It's odd, Jeff," said Norby. "I think we're getting closer to the right time, February 1, 1785, but not exactly. Perhaps we can't because you are already there, and I can't bring a *second* you to the jewelers'."

"Don't try any more, Norby." Jeff shuddered, remembering how the identical replica necklaces had tried to join together. "I don't want the two of me to merge. Something might happen."

"That's right, Jeff. You aren't an inanimate necklace. You're flesh and blood, with life and intelligence. It might short-circuit the time-fabric altogether if there were two or more of the same person close together."

"In that case, Norby, why don't you go there without me? You have never been there, so there's no problem about short-circuiting. Get into that room on February 1, 1785, right after we've been taken off to the Bastille, and leave the necklace on the floor. Boehmer and Bossange will find the necklace and think Albany dropped it. They'll be so busy delivering it to Rohan as promised, that they won't bother going to the police just to tell them there were trespassers in their office. After all, they won't have lost anything—and history will swing back to the right track."

"What does the room in the jewelers' house look like, Jeff? I don't want to make any mistakes. Not that I ever do except rarely—"

"Sure, Norby. I know how hard you *try* to be accurate."

"Are you implying—"

"Not at all. I'm just wondering if you can tune into it and go there without my help. The replica necklace is there and you can tune into that, provided you don't tune into it at a different place and in a different time."

"Exactly. That's why you've got to describe the room. I'll have to concentrate on the room as accurately as I can imagine it."

"Good. That's exactly what you'll have to do." Carefully, he described the room, trying hard not to worry about all the things that could go wrong, that could change history again, and that might leave him here in the Bastille indefinitely.

Norby said, "You aren't being very clear about the room, Jeff."

"I'm sorry, Norby, I'm thinking of other things." He tried again, clearing his mind. When he was finished he said, "And that's the best I can do. It was dark and I didn't see it clearly, and everything that was happening, all of it unexpected, threw me off."

"Well, I'll do my best." Norby placed the Queen's necklace in the light from his hat. "I hope this necklace is the solution to the time distortion problem."

"If it isn't—"

"Then I'll take you back to join Albany, Fargo, and Marcel. Then, one by one, I'll take each of you to whatever part of the new time-track on Earth we can reach without fading out."

Jeff felt more depressed than ever. "I don't really want the new time-track, Norby. I want to go back to our own world, our own ways, our own time, to all our friends and to all the other worlds we know."

"Me, too, Jeff. Good-bye."

"Norby! We're in France, and I feel blue. Please don't say good-bye because it sounds so final. Say 'au revoir' as the French do—till we see each other again."

12
The Solution

Jeff must have dozed after Norby left. He was tired enough to be able to do that even in his state of anxiety.

When he awoke, the light through the window was brighter. Clearly morning was coming. He blinked at the light, aware that his stomach was rumbling, that his throat was dry, and that there was a crick in his back from lying on lumps of straw.

But he was also reasonably warm. Suddenly, it struck him that this was odd, since the Bastille was always a cold place—

Wait! Why shouldn't he be warm? The Bastille was only cold in the winter. The first time he had been in one of the dungeons was February 1, 1785. Naturally, it would be cold then. The second time, they had arrived on July 14, 1805, in the new time-track, and, of course, it was warm then.

But then they had moved back, he had thought, near to February 1, 1785 in order to replace the Queen's necklace. It should be cold, but he was warm. Was it summer again?

And what was all that noise?

It sounded like the roar of an ocean in a storm, except that occasionally he could distinguish words. The noise poured through the window, as if hundreds, maybe thousands, of people were milling in the courtyard below.

He heard people running through the halls of the Bastille, and he clung to the grating high up in the dungeon door to see if he could tell what was going on.

Men, and women too, with grimy faces and ragged clothes were shouting and banging on doors with cudgels.

"Liberty! Equality! Brotherhood!" The words were shouted over and over in French.

"Here!" shouted Jeff. "Let me out! What's happened?"

"Down with the aristocrats," shouted a grim-faced woman, her forehead streaked with blood. "We are releasing the prisoners and tearing down the Bastille!"

Men with axes broke the locks and the prison doors were opened. There weren't many prisoners in the Bastille that day, but Jeff was one of them. And as he emerged, he understood that the day must be July 14, 1789, the first Bastille Day.

Jeff realized also, with considerable discomfort, that if Norby came back for him, the small robot would be seen by thousands of people. Yet Jeff couldn't stay in the Bastille. His liberators, in their enthusiasm, would never let him. Nor could he hide, for every cell was being systematically opened and searched.

In fact, it was too late for any evasion. He had been pulled out of the dungeon and swept along in the undertow of humanity surging through the Bastille.

Before long he was pushed and pulled out of the building, across the drawbridge, and finally into the maelstrom that was Paris at the dawn of the French Revolution.

He had lost his wig, fortunately. And his clothes were so stained and torn that he did not look like an aristocrat's servant. He certainly didn't look like a royal gentleman-in-waiting, as he had appeared on the stage of the Metropolitan Museum in Manhattan, USA sector of the Terran Federation.

"Back!" shouted a burly man. "We must tear down the Bastille stone by stone!"

The crowd surged back toward the building, carrying Jeff with it. Jeff struggled desperately to move against the flow. He did not want to go into the Bastille again, not even to pull it down.

Someone's wooden club caught him in the pit of his belly, and he doubled over, unable to breathe for a minute.

"My apologies," shouted the club's owner. "You are so tall I mistook you for one of the King's mercenaries. But you are only a boy and you have no weapon. Come, it is too dangerous for you here."

"I'm a visiting American," said Jeff. "I need to get back to the—uh—place where I've been living, so I can get my weapons. You helped us in our revolution, and I would like to help you in return."

Rough friendly hands clapped him on the back, and someone thrust a metal bar into his hand. "Well spoken, lad," said the burly man. "Now, on to the Bastille."

Jeff stumbled and fell as the crowd pushed back to the Bastille, and, for an agonizing moment, he thought he would be trampled to death. Then someone cursed and kicked him, and the kick rolled him to the side of the street, next to a wooden barrel that smelled awful. Jeff crouched behind the barrel, pretending to be unconscious.

I must calm myself, he thought. History has come back to normal again, at least as far as Bastille Day. And I'm holding a long piece of metal. It isn't a lightning rod, but I can pretend it is. I can focus my thoughts on Norby and maybe he'll rescue me.

The roaring of the crowd at the Bastille reverberated with booms like nearby thunder, as the thousands of voices shouted in defiance and triumph. It was the beginning of great changes and, although the ocean of people now on the move didn't know it, it was the beginning of terror and of wars that would last for a quarter of a century and would shape a sharply different world.

The new world that followed the wars of the French Revolution was to have its dark periods, but by Jeff's time, it had become a world of peace. To the people of Jeff's time, war was an unthinkable crime, and the Terran Federation worked hard to create a climate of hope and prosperity.

Yet it was this terrible Revolution, beginning with the fall of the Bastille, that had started the necessary chain of events.

No, thought Jeff. History says that Napoleon said it was the *necklace* that changed things, increasing the public dislike of the royal family, especially hatred of the Queen and her favorites, making the Revolution inevitable, and a constitutional monarchy impossible.

Jeff had seen both histories.

If there had been a constitutional monarchy in France, there would have been no Napoleon. But despite Napoleon's excesses, he started the modern world rolling. He inspired the Code Napoleon which revolutionized French law and was imitated by other countries. He encouraged science, forcing his adversary, Great Britain, to encourage it, too. His armies spread the new notions of revolution throughout Europe and gave all its nations a sense of nationalism. Everywhere freedom increased, even if not without trouble.

It was sad that, before the invention of nuclear weapons, war should seem to be a necessary agent for change, but that's the way it was. It was better in Jeff's time, when space exploration and colonization supplied the spur to change.

Thinking of these things, Jeff became so homesick he could hardly grasp the metal rod and tune into Norby.

"Jeff, did you have to hide behind this smelly barrel?"

Startled by the words in Terran Basic, Jeff craned his neck until he could look into the barrel. There was Norby, up to the neck of his own barrel in slop.

"What do I do, Jeff? If I rise into the air, people will see me."

"Turn your antigrav on low," said Jeff. "It will be easier to lift you out. Did you have to transport into the barrel itself, instead of behind it next to me?"

"I couldn't help it. Maybe my barrel was attracted to this barrel—"

"Not funny," said Jeff, lifting Norby. "This smells worse than anything I've ever encountered."

"Hey," yelled a man, snatching at Norby. "Some aristo has thrown his money-chest into the slop to hide it. Give it to me, boy."

Norby spun. The slop slopped all over Jeff and the man who was clutching at Norby. The man cursed. He suddenly lost interest in Norby and was swallowed up by the crowd. Jeff pulled Norby down to him, behind the slop-barrel.

"Get us out of here at once, Norby. Please!"

"Aren't you even going to thank me for taking the necklace back to the jewelers and restoring the proper time-track?"

"Thanks, Norby, I'm proud of you, but maybe you can ignore the smell more than I can. We have to get out of here, and into a lake, so we can wash this stuff off ourselves."

Jeff was wet. All wet. And unable to breathe.

Like any air-breathing animal, he swam upward, hoping that the faint gleam in the water was Norby, but unable to take the time to swim to him. Air was the first consideration.

His head broke the surface and then he realized why the water had tasted odd. He was not in a lake, but in the ocean.

Norby's barrel broke the surface of the water and then rose higher to hang over Jeff's head. Now clean, the barrel spun rapidly to force the water off its side and lid, and then the lid rose. Norby looked down at Jeff and extended an arm.

"We've had our nice bath—"

"Nice bath! I almost drowned!"

"—and I think you'd better take my arm because we should leave. It's getting crowded here."

"We're in the middle of an ocean. How can it be crowded?"

"Look in back of you."

Bearing down on them was a ship. Most of its hull was black, and part of its funnel was red. The whole thing looked as big as a skyscraper lying down on the water. It was moving fast, and Jeff could see the name of the ship.

"Queen Elizabeth Two," said Jeff. "Take me away, Norby.

114

She may have been the most beautiful ship of the 20th century, but that's not our century and—"

And then they were in the grey of hyperspace.

——I just didn't go far enough forward in time, Jeff.

——Hardly! Please try again, because I'm wet and thirsty and hungry and tired.

——I'm sorry, Jeff. All this travelling around in time and space has upset my circuits. Or maybe the stupid replica necklace was pulling at me and upsetting my calculations. Jeff, what am I going to do about that replica? I've been thinking about it and getting more and more scared.

——More and more scared about what? The replica?

——Yes! That replica gives me mysterious tingles in my vital parts. I've decided I don't really want to go near it again.

——But you must, Norby. You know you must. Fargo, Albany, and Marcel are in the far future. The Other's replica—or the defective travel device, as he called it—is there, too, so we must join it. Tune into the replica once more, Norby. Please, just once more.

——Jeff, I'm really afraid.

——There is no choice, Norby.

——But what if the replica—that dangerous travel device—does something to me. I feel worse and worse each time I'm with it. I think I have had too much contact with it.

Jeff hummed to himself so that he could think without Norby tuning into his thoughts.

——Jeff, are you angry? You know I like Fargo and Albany, and I guess Marcel Oslair is okay. I want to rescue

115

them, but I just *hate* that replica. You don't know what it feels like. If the replica keeps me in the far future, then all of us will be trapped there.

——Yes, we may be. And since the time distortion is corrected and history has been changed back, that planet isn't such a bad place to be. We'll have to chance it, Norby.

Jeff stopped trying to conceal his thought from Norby and let it out: Since history was back to normal, he and Norby could go to their own time. They could go home.

——But you don't want to do that without your brother and Albany Jones (said Norby).

——No, I don't.

——And I don't either.

Jeff felt a tremor as if hyperspace itself was vibrating, and he landed on something hard.

13
The Trap

The orange-pink ceiling seemed to smile down on Jeff as he lay flat on his back on the marble floor, but next to him was a display case that was smashed, its plasto-glass in shards all around him.

At first he thought he'd broken it in landing, but he could find no new tears in his clothing and he himself wasn't scratched.

"Welcome back to planet I-13, which is beautiful once more," said Marcel Oslair, walking toward Jeff with an arm outstretched to help him to his feet.

"Thanks, Marcel. Have you seen Norby? And where are Fargo and Albany?"

"The loving couple is there, in the garden." Marcel pointed to the window.

Jeff saw his brother and the most beautiful member of the Manhattan police force strolling together, holding hands. They were followed by a number of laughing children of a variety of species.

"When the planet returned to the normal time-track," said Marcel in French-accented Terran Basic, "the children thought our costumes hilarious. And there you can see Mentor Dickens—that seems to be the robot's name in *this* time—trying to urge the children to stop following your brother and to go to lunch."

"Ah, there's Norby!" said Jeff, carefully moving aside a section of cabinet that almost concealed Norby's barrel. The broken edges of plasto-glass were not as sharp as those of ordinary glass, but he still had to brush them aside with caution.

Norby's barrel was lying, closed up, on a fallen shelf, amid a litter of objects that had been on display. Jeff tapped Norby's lid.

"Norby?"

There was no response. No whimsical half-head popped up with metal-lidded eyes that winked at him. Jeff tried mental telepathy, but sensed nothing. Could Norby be playing some not-so-funny game? Jeff frowned in annoyance.

"One of the false necklaces is lying beside Norby," said Marcel.

"One of them? There was only one in the case when Albany arrived. She was wearing the travel device. She threw it to me, and I put it back into history. The one in the case was only a model of it, and it didn't have diamonds in it as this one does."

"Ah, but while you were gone, the big robot that is now Mentor Dickens had one of his machines put imitation diamonds in the model so that the museum would have a replica of the Queen's necklace instead of a replica of a forbidden travel device. Then Albany gave the real diamond necklace to Norby when he appeared some time ago. Did you put it back into history, too?"

"Certainly. That's what changed the time-track up here, Marcel. But I'm worried about Norby. He acts as though he

118

were in a coma of some sort and—and I'm beginning to think he's not pretending."

"I don't see anything wrong with him," said Marcel. "What about the other side—the side he's lying on?"

"Both sides are the same—," muttered Jeff, but he rolled Norby's barrel till the other side showed, and his throat tightened. This time there *was* a difference in the sides.

Marcel said excitedly, "There it is. The second replica. I hadn't finished telling you. After the museum went back to the true time-track, there were two necklaces in the case. The model of the diamond one, and the model of the travel device."

"Not a model of it," said Jeff. "That's the real travel device we're looking at, the one that's clinging to Norby. I'm sure of it."

The device looked just as it had when Jeff had buried Friend in the Paleolithic cave. It had no diamonds, but Jeff knew it had acquired false diamonds in the 18th century and had kept them right down to the moment when Albany Jones was transported from the museum stage to the jewelers' house and then to planet I-13. Jeff had taken it away, but now it had completed its circle and was back.

Norby had tuned to it and, in this fashion, had arrived here with Jeff. The device had, in turn, fastened itself to Norby somehow when he had arrived, draping itself on one side of Norby's barrel. What seemed most hideous to Jeff was that the back tassels, the ones you had to loop twice to turn the necklace into a travel device, had worked themselves inside the armholes of Norby's barrel.

It was as though Norby had tried to retract his arms into his barrel, but the tassels had stayed firmly attached to his hands. The sliding metal plates that closed the armholes when the arms were retracted were kept open a crack by the back tassels of the device, which reached inward while the rest of the device remained outside.

Jeff lifted Norby's barrel and carried it out into the hall, followed by Marcel. "I must speak to Computer General, Marcel. Please get Mentor Dickens. Get Fargo and Albany, too."

The little Frenchman was off at a run. "I know where the museum office is," he shouted. "I'll be right back."

The co-director of the museum came hastening back with Marcel. He was a human being. His brow was furrowed in concern as he looked down at the unmoving Norby. "My name is Laro Smith. Please tell me what has happened."

Fargo and Albany arrived, too, their joy at seeing Jeff turning to sudden concern over the comatose Norby. Others connected with the museum gathered—some human, some biologically alien, some robotic—and all were sympathetic as they listened to Jeff's story. This world, in the true time-track, seemed a kindly one indeed.

"So you see," said Jeff, holding Norby tightly, "we came back here in the hope that we four human beings who are alien to this world might be able to return to our own time. Norby was reluctant to come because the travel device had an unsettling effect upon him, an effect that increased with each contact. I didn't pay enough attention to that; I thought only of reaching my friends and getting them home. Now he's lying here as though he were dead and without him we can't go home. But Norby is my friend and I'd rather be here with him than at home without him. If he can be saved, I want to save him. Please put me in touch with Computer General—if there is one on this time-track."

"There is," said Mentor Dickens. "I alerted it when I was first informed there was an emergency. It will respond to you now."

The words of Computer General promptly sounded in the minds of all of them.

——Jefferson Wells, I have heard your story. You and your robot have corrected the major time distortion and all history has come back as it was and this is well.

"Yes," said Jeff impatiently, "we know that. But how do we go home now?"

——Your robot brought you here and must take you home.

"But our robot does not respond to us."

——I do not know how to make your robot operational again.

Jeff seized upon the wording. "Is it just that Norby is not operational, that he's just blocked from functioning? You mean Norby isn't actually—dead?"

——This is correct. I have scanned the robot-body and it seems that it is the travel device that is blocking him. Unfortunately, it cannot be pulled out without damaging the robot.

"Can we break the necklace—I mean the device?" asked Jeff. "Might not breaking the device put an end to its powers and leave Norby free to resume operation and take us home?"

——This might be so were it not that the special metal used by the Others to construct the device is extremely resistant to being broken or destroyed. I know of no way in which it can be done.

Fargo said, "Then we must pull it out of Norby, Jeff. If he's holding the back tassels in his hand, it shouldn't hurt him to pull them away."

Jeff shook his head. "I don't think it's that simple. Since Norby can travel through time, the Mentor robots who first constructed him must have incorporated a device inside him that is made of the same metal and has the same powers as the travel device that is now clinging to him. Different samples of the metal seem to have a powerful attraction for each other. Remember when the jewelers' device tried to join the other portion of itself that was on Albany's neck."

Albany grimaced at the memory. She said, "But that was because the jewelers' replica and my replica were actually the same object in different sections of the time-track. The replica was trying to join itself. Surely this device here and whatever is inside Norby are not identical."

Computer General's telepathic voice was sensed again.

——Both the human named Jeff and the human named Albany have portions of the truth. There is a device within Norby, one that is weaker but safer than the device now clinging to him. The two devices are not identical, but there is an attraction between them that becomes stronger each time one is tuned to the other.

"Aha," said Fargo, "Friend used it to journey to Paleolithic Earth, but after that it wasn't used again until Jeff tied it on Albany. But then Norby kept tuning to it over and over, making the attraction between it and himself stronger and stronger, until—" and Fargo pointed to the device clinging to the unconscious Norby.

At once the Computer General could be sensed again.

——That is so, but I do not know how to release your robot from this trap.

During the morning of the next day there was a brief rainstorm, but the sun came out in the afternoon and the garden sparkled as if a billion small diamonds had been thrown on the leaves and flowers. Fargo had to drag Jeff outside, where Albany was telling old Earth tales to the small nursery children, who were cared for by nurse-robots while the mothers worked in the museum.

Ever since the terraforming of planet I-13, called "Garden" by the human visitors and workers, it had been kept for growing plants useful to all oxygen-breathing species and as a universal museum center.

Jeff cared for none of this. He sat and scowled with a woebegone face—thinking—thinking—

Yet he could not think of a way out. His thoughts merely went about in circles.

Fargo, ever the optimist, said, "Come on, Jeff. If we can't go home to our own world in our own time, we'll just have to make the best of things. This is a wonderful future, and the planet is beautiful. It could be worse, couldn't it?"

Jeff said dully, "I see how it is with the rest of you. Marcel is happy here, learning robotics. Now that we know his disappearance didn't upset history, he doesn't have to go back to the Bastille to die. You and Albany could be happy here, too. You have each other and new worlds to explore and things to do. In this future, hyperdrive is common; and if you can't go home, you can visit millions of worlds if you wish. You can even visit Terra if you're content to visit it in this future time and never go back into the proper time in which you belong."

Fargo nodded. "Well? And doesn't all this apply to you, too, little brother?"

"No," said Jeff. "I want to go home. I want to keep on being a cadet at the Space Academy. I want to be part of the early stages of space exploration. I want to contribute my part to the history of my time. Besides, you don't understand. I want Norby. I want him even more than I want my own time."

Albany had now joined them. She glanced from Jeff to Fargo and then asked the latter, "Won't he accept the situation?"

Slowly, Fargo shook his head.

Albany sat down next to Jeff and put her arm about his shoulder. "Jeff dear. I want to go home, too. My father will live out his life never knowing what happened to me, and he and my mother will both suffer so much. Do you think I want that? But we are here and we can't change it."

Jeff said angrily, "But how do you know we can't? Have you thought of everything?"

"I've tried. If Norby remains in his trap and can't be released, then we are forever imprisoned in *our* trap. We are in this far future time and here we must stay. Face it."

"*If* Norby remains in this trap. *If!*"

"No ifs about it, I'm afraid," said Fargo softly. "You've sat with Norby for over a day, Jeff, and he doesn't respond. And when you tried to tug the necklace away gently, it wouldn't come. And when you tried to bend the metal of the necklace it wouldn't bend. Nothing will make Norby work and nothing will make that travel device work, and there's nothing else in the Universe, even in this amazingly technological far

124

future, that will move us through time. So what is there to do?"

"You two are giving up," said Jeff between his teeth, "but I'm never going to give up. I'm going to act as though there's hope, because if I don't, then I may miss some opportunity for finding a solution. What's happened to our costumes, by the way? We'll need them when I figure out a way to get back home. And don't worry, I'll figure a way yet!"

That day, all three of the Terrans were wearing the simple, flowing garments of the time. Jeff was distantly aware of the pleasure of feeling clean, but he did not find it either a consolation or a compensation for the trap they were in. "Well, where are they?" he repeated.

"Don't get excited, Jeff," said Fargo. "The robots cleaned them, mended yours—which badly needed it—and put them on display in the museum. If you hadn't been spending all your time with Norby, you'd have seen them."

Jeff turned and ran into the museum. Fargo was right—the costumes were there next to a display case containing the model of the Queen's necklace. He studied them for a while and then went to the small room where Norby was being kept. He sat down next to his robot, touching Norby and trying to make contact.

Jeff thought, Maybe there's some way of making the Norby-necklace combination work as a time-travel device.

He put his hands on the necklace as it hung on Norby's barrel, and he concentrated until he was in almost a trance. But even in the trance, his concentration wasn't complete, since he kept interrupting himself with one sharp realization. Even if he found himself home, what good would it be if he couldn't free Norby?

And then he became dimly aware of Marcel standing

before him and gazing at him sadly. Jeff looked up and realized that it was twilight outside and that the museum lighting had strengthened to compensate.

Marcel, aware of Jeff's attention, said mournfully, "Ah, my good, young friend. What would I not do to help you, if I only knew how."

Jeff said, "Thanks, Marcel. You need not assure me of this. I know you would help, if you could. I haven't seemed to hit on any way of either using or saving Norby. Of course, I would rather save him—even if it meant I could never use him again."

"I understand." Marcel sat down beside Jeff and patted Norby's lid. "He is more than an automation. He is a friend; a stubborn, but a very courageous friend."

"Yes, that he is," said Jeff, unable to pay much attention.

Marchel said, "Computer General says Norby is alive, does it not?"

"Yes, but if I can't get through to Norby, it's as if he's dead."

" 'As if' is not the thing itself, Jeff. I have heard from Albany that you berated her and Fargo for giving up hope, and you must not do so yourself. Perhaps Norby can hear you, but cannot respond. Perhaps—since he is not dead—he is trying to adjust himself—his—his gears, or whatever it is that composes him. If you could help him, somehow, in his effort—"

Jeff looked up sharply. "You mean instead of my trying to concentrate on getting a response from him, I should concentrate on giving him some sort of response from *me*."

"That is what I think. Since he can't get to you, you must get to him."

"And if I do get to him, I might somehow help him make one of the two time-travel devices work, the replica or whatever it is inside himself."

"Yes. Yet even if you can make him travel in time and take you back to your home—it will not help you liberate Norby, will it? If the people of this far future time cannot free Norby, then the people of your less-far-future time will not be able to, will they?"

"Of course my time would not know, but I am not concerned about that." Jeff's eyes were suddenly shining with determination. "I'll help him move me, but I won't go into the past. I'll go still farther into the future where technology may have developed even further. If I should disappear, Marcel, tell the others I will try to be back soon."

Marcel nodded eagerly. "My best wishes to you, my good friend," he said and he left.

Jeff held Norby tightly to his chest and for the first time since he had discovered Norby in his coma, he relaxed. He was not going to try to pull Norby's consciousness out of him; he was going to try, telepathically, to push his own human consciousness into the little robot—surely an easier task.

——Norby. I know you're in the grip of that defective travel device, but don't give up. I'm going to concentrate on something and I want you, if you can sense my thoughts, to concentrate on the same thing. Think as hard as you ever have, because we need all the power we can get to break the grip of that horrible object on your barrel.

Jeff visualized. The picture in his mind grew sharper and sharper until, finally, it blotted out everything else but the conviction that Norby was alive and could help.

——Help yourself, Norby.

And with all the force of his imagination, Jeff broadcast another thought; not to Norby this time.

——You Others, out there somewhere, help me!

14
The Power of the Necklace

"Where am I?" asked Jeff.

"In the Cavern of Thought, time-traveller. Be welcome."

The speaker was the tallest being in the room, and the room was a purple rock cavern lit by small, luminous creatures that clung to projecting points of stone. In the center of the floor was a copper-colored space shaped like a comet, and Jeff had landed on the head of it.

The tall speaker, dressed in purple robes the color of the cavern, was one of three Others who looked at Jeff with their three eyes shining in the strange light. Their lower arms were folded in majestic dignity, while the top arms of each were outstretched, the hands cupping hollow balls made of a lacework of metal that was dull in color, just like the metal of the necklace that was holding Norby in paralysis.

"You are Others," said Jeff. "I needed help and I concentrated on making the travel device find you. It was your workmanship that made the two devices, the one in my robot and the one that now has power over him. If anyone can release my robot it will be you."

And yet, even as he spoke, Jeff felt discouraged, for he could see no sign in the cavern of a suitably high technology. Had he moved mistakenly into the past—or into a future in which the Others had degenerated—forgotten—lost their abilities?

The Others said nothing for what seemed to Jeff many minutes, and then they held the metal balls higher in their outstretched upper arms. Instantly, a dark purple flying creature, like a bird with two sets of wings and a snakelike neck, flew out of the cave shadows, picked up the three balls in its beak and two talons, and flew back again out of sight. The Others folded their upper arms and nodded.

"We know your history, Jefferson Wells," said the tallest Other. "Computer General exists in this time, though in greatly expanded form as compared with the time during which you met it. It has the records and we knew you would reach us, though we did not know when, nor that it would be through your own choice."

"Compared to the time in which I knew Computer General, is this the future?"

"The far future. So far that your sun is now a red giant. This much we can tell you because even in your day it was predicted. What's more, you human beings knew the change would take place very slowly, so that there was time for the human species to settle elsewhere and be safe."

"But do you use only Computer General? I see no robots, no machines—"

"There are robots. Not here, but on most planets. We do not use Computer General except for information. Computer General uses us. We are specialized in a certain kind of thinking you would call intuition and insight. All biological intelligence is capable of this, and some robots are as well, but we have specialized in it for millennia. We Others are the oldest of all the intelligent species in the Universe."

"Can you free my robot from this terrible device that has trapped him?"

"We do not know."

"But you're the wisest of all—"

"We did not say that, young human being. We try to be wise; that is all. There are many forms of wisdom, helped by many things, including human emotion."

"How can my emotion help my wisdom?" demanded Jeff.

"You love your robot, don't you?"

"Yes, I do."

"And your love will strengthen and lengthen your concentration and make you capable of reaching your robot, when, without love, it would not."

"Shall I try now?"

"Yes. And we will help. We will link with you. The device was one of the mistakes of our species long ago, and we must try to help rid the Universe of it. Stand up, Jefferson Wells, and we will touch you while you hold Norby."

Jeff stood tall on the metal representation of a comet, Norby in his arms. He closed his eyes and felt hands being placed on his chest and back, one by one. He counted to twelve and that was all. The Others were very close, and he did not dare to open his eyes for fear that the sight of them would make him lose all concentration on Norby.

Norby! Suddenly, Jeff knew that Norby would help—just as he had helped to get Jeff to this far distant future.

Time, thought Jeff. All the circles complete. No more need. No more power. Let go. Let go. Let—

He could sense a shower of particles falling to the ground, but it wasn't rain. The pressure of the twelve hands vanished and he opened his eyes to see the Others standing back, staring at Jeff's feet. He looked down.

Fine metal was scattered all over, but at a gesture from the

131

Others, it all began to move, coalescing into a ball just in front of Jeff. The tallest Other stepped forward, scooped up the ball in one of his lower hands, and smiled at Jeff.

"Useful stuff, this metal. It came from the Universe before this one. We can use it again."

"And don't make a mistake this time!" shouted Norby, all four of his eyes blinking with outrage. "Don't make a dangerous travel device with it! Use it wisely, you dolts!"

Jeff hugged Norby and said, "Don't be offended by his remarks. He's really glad you rescued him—"

"We merely helped," said the leading Other. "You did it, Jefferson Wells. And the robot's angry remark is perfectly correct. We must use the metal wisely, and we will. This Universe will someday come to an end and the metal will help us find another. Thank you for adding to our small store of it."

The leading Other bowed to Jeff. "And now you must return to your own time."

"With a short stop at I-13 to pick up Fargo and Albany," said Jeff. "Good-bye, Others. I'm glad I met—"

But Norby, with a sound that resembled a human grinding his teeth, jumped through time and space.

Dressed in their costumes, Fargo, Albany, and Jeff stood together, Jeff holding onto Norby with his other hand. Albany was wearing the museum's model of the Queen's necklace. It was not, of course, made of the same metal as the dangerous replica that had carried her to I-13, but Mentor Dickens said the experts of Jeff's time wouldn't notice the difference. Norby had his sensor wire extended to touch an outlet connecting him to Computer General.

132

"Norby," said Fargo, tugging at his pants, because in spite of the patching, they were still too tight, "you had better be grateful to Jeff. He kept on hoping when Albany and I had given up. He would not let go of you because he loved you."

"It took him long enough," said Norby. "But I love him despite his shortcomings, because I am a loving as well as a lovable robot."

"So I see," said Fargo dryly, while Jeff smiled because Norby sounded completely himself.

Albany said, "Are you certain you can get us back to the Metropolitan Museum's stage immediately after we disappeared, Norby?"

"Not immediately. One second later. I can't go back to a time when I was still there, and it took me a second to decide you'd time-travelled and that I should hunt for you. But I doubt if anyone in the audience will notice. They may sense a tiny flicker."

"You've never been that accurate, Norby," said Fargo.

"I am now. I think I am. Contact with that other travel device gave me more power to be accurate, and to take more than one person with me at a time. Its power leaked to me. Of course it was an evil and dangerous power, but the evil and danger didn't leak to me because I am so virtuous."

"And modest," said Fargo.

"Will it help you in your travels through space?" asked Albany.

Norby thought. "No. Just through time. I can haul all of you through space but there's room for only one within my personal field. The rest would not be able to breathe if we weren't in a suitable atmosphere."

"But we have to go through space to get to Earth. Through

space as well as through time, don't we?" asked Albany. "Will it be safe for us to do that?"

"Yes," said Jeff. "Computer General is going to augment Norby's power. We must do it all at once instead of in three stages, to keep the return from being noticed. We've been trying to keep Norby's time-travel ability a secret."

"Then let's go," said Fargo. "As long as we can get back to Terra, there are friends I would like to see, much as I will miss this beautiful world."

"Good-bye," said Marcel Oslair wistfully. "My whole life has been made fortunate by my meeting with you in the Bastille, my friends, and though I am happy with this beautiful world, there will never be a minute in which I will forget you. And I will make my own little robot like Norby."

"Not like me," said Norby. "Nothing is like me."

"And I wish to say good-bye," said Mentor Dickens. "Marcel and I are studying the French Revolution together, including the novel by Charles Dickens, after whom I am named. I am glad that I am not the Mentor robot I would have become if you had not corrected the time distortion. I like being able to smile and to work and to study with biological creatures."

"Good-bye!"

"Good-bye!"

The return to the stage of the museum was not obvious, merely embarrassing, for they were all on the floor, Albany's huge skirt spread out. They were all still holding hands, with a silvery barrel in Jeff's lap.

The audience laughed.

Fargo's thought went out to the others:

——Play it for laughs.

There was a devil-may-care smile on his handsome face that did not in the least resemble that of Louis the Sixteenth.

Albany smiled and patted down the front of her skirt before it had a chance to reveal that she was not wearing long pantaloons.

"Sire," she said, "truly this diamond necklace will cause trouble in our realm, since it seems to turn things upside down. I begin to believe that upside down is the natural state of things, and that Jacques could demonstrate that his automaton can even dance upside down."

——Jeff, I don't have to, do I?

——You'd better. We want to keep the audience's mind off what really happened.

——But my arms come out of the sides of my barrel. I'll have to hop from one hand to the other and I may fall—

——Just use a touch of antigrav and you'll be as graceful as a bird, Norby. Dance, while the audience is still laughing.

Fargo's thoughts added:

——And before the director comes out on stage and tries to murder us all.

Norby danced on his hands. It was not graceful, but, as Jeff reflected, anything to keep them laughing.

On his next vacation from Space Academy, Jeff visited the Metropolitan Museum with Norby, who was strangely silent as they stared at the "Queen's Necklace," which was labelled as the replica made by Boehmer and Bossange.

"Nobody will ever know it's not the real replica," said

135

Norby, "and that it's only a copy made by Mentor Dickens. This necklace can't go anywhere or anytime—but the one inside me can."

Norby jiggled on his feet. "I rescued history, didn't I, Jeff?"

"You sure did, Norby."

"You helped, of course."

"A little."

Norby put one hand on the display case and the other on his barrel. There was an odd noise, as if he were clearing his speech mechanism, and then, in a deeper voice, Norby spoke:

"It was a far, far better thing I did—"

"Norby!"